18.95

The Collector's Wodehouse

P. G. WODEHOUSE

Do Butlers
Burgle Banks?

THE OVERLOOK PRESS
WOODSTOCK & NEW YORK

This edition first published in the United States in 2005 by
The Overlook Press, Peter Mayer Publishers, Inc.
Woodstock and New York

WOODSTOCK
One Overlook Drive
Woodstock, NY 12498
www.overlookpress.com
[for individual orders, bulk and special sales, contact our Woodstock office]

NEW YORK
141 Wooster Street
New York, NY 10012

First published 1968
Copyright © 1968 by P. G. Wodehouse

Cataloging-in-Publication Data is available from the Library of Congress

Manufactured in Germany

ISBN 1-58567-747-7

1 3 5 7 9 8 6 4 2

Do Butlers
Burgle Banks?

CHAPTER 1

Charlie Yost, the Chicago gunman, called on Horace Appleby one morning in June as he chatted with Basher Evans before going off to the Wellingford races.

Ferdie announced him.

'Charlie's here, guv'nor,' he said, and Horace frowned. He was displeased with this hand across the sea and wished to have nothing more to do with him.

Horace Appleby was the head of the Appleby gang, well known and respected in criminal circles, and Charlie, who for various reasons had felt it wiser to leave Chicago for the time being and transfer his activities to England, had been one of his boys. In his long and prosperous career Horace had always had to depend very much on those who worked for him – Basher Evans, for instance, expert at opening safes, and Ferdie the Fly, who, while definitely not of the intelligentsia, had the invaluable gift of being able to climb up the side of any house you placed before him, using only toes, fingers and personal magnetism. Horace himself played the role of a General in time of war, planning campaigns at the base and leaving his troops to carry them out.

He and his boys were a happy family, and in his dealings with them he strove always to be the kindly father, liking to see them doing well and taking a benevolent pleasure in handing them their cut after each successful coup. But if occasion arose, he could be a stern parent. Charlie Yost had carried a gun with him when on duty, and in the matter of guns Horace's views were rigid. He would not permit them, and of this prejudice of his Charlie had been perfectly well aware. But he had flouted his leader's authority and retribution had been swift. With a firm hand Horace had held up his latest cut, refusing to give him even a token wage.

So now he frowned. He resented having his privacy invaded by employees whom he had struck off his payroll. He also felt a little nervous. Charlie, informed that he was not to receive any reward for his services, had made no secret of his dissatisfaction, and he was presumably still carrying that gun. A man of his impulsive temperament, taught at his mother's knee to shoot first and argue afterwards, might well take it into his head to open the negotiations by saying it with bullets.

'May as well see him, guv'nor,' said Basher, reading his thoughts. 'He won't start anything, not while I'm here.'

Horace looked at him, and saw what he meant. There was only one adjective to be applied to Llewellyn ('Basher') Evans, and it was one which would have sprung automatically to the lips of any resident of Hollywood – the adjective colossal. Though he was impressively tall, it was not his cubits that filled the beholder with awe so much as his physical development. Wherever a man could bulge with muscle, he bulged. He even bulged in places where one would not have expected him to bulge. The clothes he wore had presumably been constructed by a tailor, but it was hard to believe that he could have been adequately fitted out by anyone less spacious in his methods than Omar the Tent Maker.

The scrutiny convinced Horace that with this colossus beside him he had nothing to fear from the most disgruntled gunman.

'Very well,' he said. 'Bring him in, Ferdie,' and a moment later Charlie entered.

An impression exists in the public mind that there is some system of rules and regulations, rigidly enforced by the men up top, which compels all American gangsters to look like Humphrey Bogart and when speaking to snarl like annoyed cougars. Should one of them fail to meet these requirements, it is supposed, he is placed in the centre of a hollow square of sinister characters with names like Otto the Ox and Beef Stroganoff and formally stripped of his Homburg hat and trench coat.

Actually, however, a considerable latitude is permitted, and the rank and file may indulge their personal tastes without incurring any sort of penalty.

Charlie Yost, to take a case in point, was a pleasant, soft-spoken little man with an inoffensive face rendered additionally inoffensive by large horn-rimmed spectacles. Meeting him on the street you would have set him down as a minor unit in some commercial firm or possibly a clerk in a lawyer's office, never suspecting him of being a man of violence.

Nor, indeed, was he, except when the necessity arose of liquidating some business competitor, and this he did not look on as violence but simply as routine inseparable from commerce. He was rather a sentimental man, who subscribed to homes for unwanted dogs and cats and rarely failed to cry when watching a motion picture with a sad ending.

Horace, fortified by the presence of Basher, greeted him coldly.

'Well, Yost?'

Usually Horace's majesty, so different from anything he had ever encountered in Chicago, overawed Charlie, but such was the magnitude of his grievance that he did not quail before it now. Speaking with equal coldness and out of the left side of his mouth, a thing he never did except when greatly moved, he said:

'I want that money.'

'What money?'

'The money you owe me.'

Horace drew himself to his full height. Even when full, it was not a very high height, but he managed to make the gesture impressive. Napoleon had the same knack.

'I owe you nothing,' he said. 'You knew my rules when you entered my organization. You were told in simple words that I do not permit the carrying of guns. You wilfully disobeyed me and I imposed a salutary fine upon you. There is nothing more to say. Basher, show Mr Yost out.'

'Come along, Charlie,' said Basher, and Charlie gave him a long, thoughtful stare.

Actually, Llewellyn Evans was a mild man, the sobriquet of Basher having been bestowed on him not because he bashed but because he looked so like one who on the slightest provocation would bash. But as there was nothing in his appearance to indicate that he was not a menace to pedestrians and traffic, Charlie, as he had predicted, made no move in the direction of what he had called starting something. He allowed himself to be escorted peacefully to the door. Turning there and speaking quietly but with menace, he said:

'I'll be seeing you.'

And on this significant speech he withdrew.

Basher came back into the room, to find Horace's composure

quite restored. These little disturbances never ruffled him for long.

'He's gone,' he said. 'And you'd better be going, too, guv'nor, or you'll be missing your train.'

'You're perfectly right, Basher,' said Horace. 'And that would not do at all. I've a couple of tips on the two-thirty and the three o'clock and am confidently expecting to clean up.'

And so saying he went off to catch the express to Wellingford, where, though he was not aware of it, he would meet Mike Bond, Ada Cootes, Jill Willard, Sergeant Claude Potter of Scotland Yard and others who were to play an important part in his affairs.

So true it is that in this life we never know what may be waiting for us around the next corner.

CHAPTER 2

I

Having dictated in his pleasant voice half a dozen letters of not remarkable interest, Mike Bond paused, seeming to have fallen into a coma, and Ada Cootes took advantage of the lull to look up from her notebook and inspect her surroundings. This was the first time she had been inside Mallow Hall, her secretarial work up to the present having been confined to office hours at the bank, and its opulence filled her with awe. She had heard much about its splendours from her friend Jill Willard, the nurse who was there in attendance on Mike's Aunt Isobel, but like the Queen of Sheba she felt that the half had not been told her.

Mallow Hall was one of the show places of Worcestershire, the home for four centuries of the Armitage family and purchased from the last of the clan by the late Sir Hugo Bond of Bond's Bank. It stood, gracious and Elizabethan, in the midst of spreading parkland not far from the market town of Wellingford in the Vale of Evesham, and the thought uppermost in Ada's mind was that it must have cost Sir Hugo a fortune. Not that that would have worried that legendary man. The rule by which he had always lived was that the best would have to do till something better came along.

The room in which they were sitting, Ada presumed, was the old man's study. Everything in it was impressively large – the desk, the chairs, the fireplace, the portrait of a rubicund Sir Hugo in hunting costume above it, the grandfather clock and the cupboard in the corner by the window. Only the occupants were not on the heroic scale. Ada herself was short and stocky, Mike slim and wiry. He rode a good deal, and in his under-graduate days at Cambridge had been a lightweight boxer of distinction.

He had recently succeeded his Uncle Hugo as owner and manager of Bond's Bank, one of those substantial country banks which are handed down from father to son – or, as in this case, from uncle to nephew – through the ages, growing more prosperous with each transference. He had not particularly wanted to become a banker, but Sir Hugo had been a bachelor and he his nearest relative, and he had felt it his duty to carry on the family tradition.

His silence had lasted so long that Ada began to feel con-cerned. She was devoted to Mike, and watching over him like a combined nanny and mother she had not failed to notice the change that had come over him since Sir Hugo's death. He had lost all the gaiety which had enlivened their days at the office together. Strange, felt Ada, and disquieting.

The door opened and Coleman, the Hall butler, came in.

'Excuse me, sir,' he said, with the apologetic air of one bringing bad news. 'Some ladies have arrived.'

Mike came out of his trance and stared at him blankly.

'Ladies?'

'*Six* in number, sir. I gather that they wish to borrow Sir Hugo's portrait.'

'For the statue they're putting up in the market square,

Mr Michael,' said Ada helpfully. 'The sculptor has to copy it. You remember Lady Pinner wrote about it the other day.'

Mike transferred his blank gaze to her.

'Did she?'

'Last week. Representing the Wellingford Women's Association. She said the committee had voted for it unanimously. I suppose this is the committee. You must go and see them.'

'Must I?'

'Yes,' said Ada, who could be very firm when firmness was required, and Mike went out, his despondency noticeably increased. Some men would have been overjoyed at an opportunity of a chat with six members of a Women's Association committee, but it was plain that he was not of their number.

Ada returned to her meditations. One of the letters she had taken down, she recalled, the only one that had stirred her imagination, had been to a Mr J. B. Richards of the firm of Richards, Price and Gregory, asking for a meeting to discuss a matter of the utmost urgency, which seemed to suggest that some financial problem had arisen in connection with the bank. Though this was hard to credit, for the stability of Bond's Bank was a byword throughout the county and even further.

She was still turning over these disturbing things in her mind, when her reverie was interrupted by the entry of someone much more worth looking at than Coleman the butler – Jill Willard, to wit.

Ada was glad to see her. Her friendship with Jill had begun in the mystery novels section of the library presented to the town by Sir Hugo Bond, where they had discovered a mutual taste for this form of literature, and had ripened rapidly. She now knew all that there was to be known about her – born the daughter of an impecunious squire in the west country;

educated, as they say in *Who's Who*, privately; lessening the pressure on the paternal bank account at an early age by leaving home and going off to train as a nurse, and now making a modest income in that profession.

'Why, hullo, Jill,' she said. 'Are you off duty?'

'Just having a breather. Coleman told me you were in here.'

'How are you getting on with Miss Bond?'

'Fine.'

'I'd heard she was rather a tartar.'

'Not with me. We're like a couple of sailors on shore leave. But what are you doing here?'

'Mr Michael had some letters he wanted to get off.'

'On a Saturday afternoon?'

'I didn't mind. He's so awfully nice.'

It was a pronouncement with which at one time Jill would whole-heartedly have agreed. Until recently her relations with Mike had been more than cordial, but of late a coolness had crept into them, bringing resentment with it. There was a chill in her voice as she said:

'Oh, is he?'

'Considerate and all that, I mean. He apologized for about ten minutes for wanting me to work on Saturday afternoon.'

'The least he could have done.'

'He thought I might have been planning to go to the Wellingford races.'

'Were you?'

'Certainly not,' said Ada primly. 'Still, you can't say it wasn't nice of him.'

'Perfectly sweet.'

Ada lowered her voice to a cautious undertone. 'You know, Jill, there's something the matter with Mr Michael.'

'Cold coming on?'

'No, really, I mean it. He's been quite different lately. I noticed it soon after Sir Hugo died. Before that he was always so cheerful and jolly. When I brought him his tea in the afternoon we used to have all sorts of talks.'

'What about?'

'Oh, everything. Buns.'

'Buns?'

'The ones I made for him. Saying how much he liked them. But he never mentions them now. He's worried all the time, as if he were brooding on something. Something to do with the bank it must be.'

'Why should he worry about the bank? It's like getting all concerned about Standard Oil.'

'You don't think there's anything wrong with it?'

'Of course not. How could there be?'

'Well, something's bothering him.'

'Guilty conscience, probably.'

For the first time it seemed to dawn on Ada that her friend did not share the enthusiasm she felt for her employer.

'Don't you *like* Mr Michael?' she asked, surprised.

'Not much,' said Jill, and as she spoke Coleman entered to say that Miss Bond would be glad if Miss Willard would step up and see her.

'Something wrong?'

'Miss Bond desired me to say that she is having difficulties with her crossword puzzle.'

'That's bad,' said Jill. 'Yes, that wants looking into. All right, I'll go up.'

She went out. A climb of two flights of stairs took her to the bedroom looking out over the park where Miss Isobel was confined with a broken leg, the result of a recent motoring accident.

II

The invalid was lying in bed with a dachshund and two cats to keep her company. She was an imperious old lady who looked as if forty years ago she must have been extremely handsome, though even in those days formidable. She intimidated most of those who knew her, but to Jill she had fortunately taken a fancy from the start, and their relations, as Jill had told Ada, had always been of the best. It was with only the mildest tinge of rebuke in her voice that she said:

'So there you are at last.'

Jill patted her hand affectionately.

'I came as quick as I could, sergeant major. You caught me without my spiked shoes and running shorts. I hear you've got stuck in your crossword puzzle. Anything I can do to help?'

'Don't bother. I've given it up. Those clues are too deep for me. Twelve across – "School after a break is blooming." I ask you. And all the others just as bad. The extraordinary thing is that next week there'll be a list of half-a-dozen people who got it right to the last drop, and they'll all be people who live in Leeds and Huddersfield and places like that.'

'They're brainier up there.'

'I've decided to ignore the damned thing. Life's too short. I'll have another go at that book you brought me from the library yesterday.'

'Is it any good? I picked it because I liked the title.'

'Depends what you call good. It's about a young man named

Torquil who's trying to make up his mind whether or not to be psychoanalysed. Sometimes he thinks he will, and then sometimes he thinks he won't.'

'Well, what more can you ask in the way of suspense?'

'I don't want suspense. I want a good honest love story with trembling lips and shining eyes and heaving bosoms, the lot. But the boys aren't writing that sort any more, curse them. By the way, talking of love, how are you and young Mike coming along?'

Just how her most intimate and private affairs had become revealed to this patient of hers Jill could never remember, but Miss Bond was one of those penetrating old ladies from whom nothing remains hidden for long. One day, quite unexpectedly, she had shown herself in full possession of the facts, and her talk was always apt to take, as now, an embarrassing turn.

'We aren't,' Jill said briefly.

Miss Bond's eyebrows rose.

'Lovers' tiff?'

'We don't see enough of each other these days to have tiffs.'

'He seems to be avoiding you?'

'As much as he can.'

'And when you meet, is he nervous and embarrassed?'

'I suppose you could call it that.'

'Then I see what's happened. He's trying to work up his courage to propose. Men get that way when the balloon's about to go up. They're afraid they'll be turned down. I've seen Hugo like that a dozen times when he was a young man. Tied himself into knots. And as they always did turn him down, he might just as well have saved himself all that anguish and improved his mind with a good book. What Mike's hoping is that if he goes on dithering long enough, you'll get fed up and make the first move.'

'Propose to him?'

'Why not?'

'And what do I do when he droops his eyes and falters "I'm sorry, so so sorry, but it cannot be. We can only be dear, dear friends"? Redden and go to Africa?'

'You think he'd do that?'

'His manner suggests it.'

'Cooling off, you feel?'

'That's the impression I get.'

'The boy's an idiot. What does he want? Looks? He won't find anyone prettier than you. Disposition? He must know by this time that any gairl who could stand me as long as you have has all the qualities needed to make a perfect wife.'

'Except one.'

'What's that?'

'Money,' said Jill bitterly. 'I think it's suddenly dawned on him that if he's not careful, he'll find himself saddled with a penniless wife, and he feels he can do better.'

Miss Bond was shocked.

'Mike's not like that.'

'No?'

'Of course he isn't. There's nothing mercenary about Mike. If he's behaving strangely, it's probably something to do with the bank.'

'That's what Ada thinks.'

'Who's Ada?'

'Ada Cootes, his secretary.'

'Oh, that one. I've met her. Nice gairl. Well, she's right.'

'She isn't. You're both wrong. Mine's the correct solution.'

'It's not.'

'It is.'

'Oh, hell. Of all the pigheaded gairls I ever met, you're the worst. Go and get me a whisky and soda.'

'Will the doctor approve?'

'He won't know,' said Miss Bond.

III

Mike, having got rid of the ladies' committee, came back to the study. He looked at his watch.

'We won't do any more today, Ada,' he said. 'I've kept you too late already. Thanks for being so patient. I'll drive you home.'

'Oh, Mr Michael, please.'

'No trouble.'

'No, really. It's only a mile.'

'Two.'

'Well, two. And it's a lovely evening. I'd really rather walk.'

'You're sure? Don't forget the races are on. You might run into some tough customers.'

Ada bridled a little. Her pride had been wounded.

'Thank you, Mr Michael, I can take care of myself,' she said with the quiet confidence of a girl who in her time had twice found it necessary to quell intoxicated citizens with her umbrella and had done it with the greatest success, leaving the inebriates wondering dreamily what had hit them. Though small, she was solid and muscular and when armed with this Excalibur of hers feared no foe in or out of shining armour. Her strong wrists could always be relied on to supply the follow through which makes all the difference.

It was consequently with no trepidation that she set out for the town. It was, as she had said, a lovely evening, and she found the two-mile walk most invigorating. And she had turned into the side street where her home was, a two-roomed flat over a confectioner's shop, when her thoughts were abruptly diverted by a spectacle fortunately rare in Wellingford even in race week. A few yards in front of her a stout man who looked like a Roman emperor had paused and taken his wallet from his pocket, apparently in order to gloat over its contents, and a lean predatory individual, appearing from nowhere as is the way of lean predatory individuals all the world over, had snatched it from his grasp and was now approaching her at a high rate of speed.

Except for the two intoxicated citizens of whom mention has been made, Ada's had been a sheltered life, and until now no situation of this kind had thrust itself upon her, but a woman's instinct told her the correct course to pursue. Acting promptly, as Joan of Arc would have done in her place, she extended the umbrella which had served her so well on those previous occasions. The predatory one, receiving it between his flying legs, performed several steps of what might have been one of the more uninhibited modern dances, and the wallet flew from his hand. Prudently not pausing, he continued his headlong course, and the Roman emperor, galloping up, swooped on his property and clutched it to his bosom.

In this dramatic fashion did Fate bring together Ada Cootes and Horace Appleby, whose paths would otherwise have been most unlikely to cross. Fate is always doing that sort of thing.

IV

Horace stood transfixed, still clutching the wallet. It was swollen as if with elephantiasis, for he had, as he had expected, done well on the two-thirty and the three o'clock, and the thought of how but for Ada he would have lost it rendered him mellow with gratitude. Profitable enterprises over the years had made him a rich man, though prudence led him not to flaunt his wealth but to live in a semi-detached villa in a London suburb, and like so many rich men he was careful with his money. It would have cut him to the quick to lose that wallet.

He started to thank his benefactress. Words poured from him in a steady stream, while the object of his encomiums stood blushing and drawing arabesques on the pavement with her foot.

Horace, as we have said, was careful with his money. Nevertheless he felt justified in spending it freely by way of return to this admirable girl for the good fight she had fought against the powers of darkness. With the feeling that even if her tastes lay in the direction of champagne he must do the square thing, he said:

'And now, madam, if you have no urgent engagements, I think we would both like a little something after all this excitement. Might I persuade you to join me?'

It was only with a powerful effort that Ada stopped herself from saying 'Coo!'. The word was rising to her lips when just in time she recognized it as unsuitable and substituted for it the more elegant 'Oo, thanks. I should love it.'

'Capital,' said Horace. 'Capital. There's a bar round the corner,' he added, and Ada shivered at the licentious suggestion. Not only her mother but both her aunts had warned her never,

never to go into bars. What went on in such places she had yet to learn, but she had formed a vague picture of something resembling Saturday night in the Casbah or one of those orgies which got Babylon such a bad name. Alternatively she proposed a tea shoppe, of which there were four in the High Street, and Horace accepted the amendment with relief. Champagne is not served in tea shoppes.

Seated later at a yellow table with blue humming-birds on it in a corner of the Copper Kettle, the tea pot and plate of cakes before them, the conversation flowing freely and the cakes not half bad, though well below the standard of Ada's home-mades, Horace put the question which had been puzzling him since his arrival on the race train that morning.

'Tell me something, Miss Cootes,' he said. 'Why is everything in this town Bond? The Bond Library, the Bond Hospital, the Bond this, the Bond that. I was half expecting the turf accountant with whom I did my business this afternoon to say he was the Bond Bookie. Who is this Bond of whom I hear so much?'

Ada's reply, though prompt, was not too lucid.

'Oh, that's the bank. But he's dead.'

'I beg your pardon?'

'Sir Hugo Bond. He passed on a month or so ago.'

Horace said that all flesh was as grass, and Ada agreed that there was a resemblance.

'But why do you call him the bank?' asked Horace, still puzzled.

'He owned it. While he was alive, of course.'

'Of course,' said Horace, feeling that this was reasonable.

'His nephew owns it now. Mr Michael. I'm his secretary. It was Sir Hugo who paid for all those libraries and things.

He was always doing good works about the place. Any time they wanted anything in the town they had only to ask Sir Hugo.'

'Nice fellow. Must have been rich.'

'Oh, he was. Bond's Bank makes mints of money. Why, besides putting up libraries and things he bought Mallow Hall. There's a village called Mallow about two miles from the town. That's where the Hall is. It used to belong to a Judge, a Sir something Armitage. I don't know if you've ever heard of him?'

Horace had indeed heard of him. It was only eighteen months ago that Sir Roger Armitage had sentenced a friend of his named Ginger Moffat to five years' penal servitude.

'Yes,' he said, 'the name seems familiar.'

'I was up at the Hall this afternoon doing letters for Mr Michael. You ought to see it. A regular palace.'

'Big, eh?'

'Enormous. Acres of gardens and miles of park. Sir Hugo was like that. Didn't care how much he spent.'

There was no question that she had enchained Horace's interest. He was listening now without missing a word. He and his boys specialized in forays against the country houses of the rich, and in all such enterprises it is half the battle to have a representative of the firm on the premises. It was Horace's practice to obtain the post of butler at these establishments in order to pave the way for Ferdie and the others, and he seldom found it a thing difficult to do, for his was an appearance and deportment so butlerine that few householders, seeing him, ever hesitated to welcome him in, stopping short only of laying down the red carpet.

His baldness and stoutness were what spoke to the depths of

these country house owners. Butlers, of course, come in all sizes and shapes and many an employer has to put up with a tall thin one or one with a full head of hair, but all the time he feels that there is something lacking and finds himself wishing wistfully that the agency could have sent him a major domo bulgier in the middle and thinner on top. Horace Appleby was just right. Lord Wantagh (of the Wantagh diamonds) and Sir Rupert Finch (of the Finch pearls) and others into whose orbit he had flitted had all been convinced that they had got a treasure. Actually, of course, though they were not to know it, it was the other way round. It was Horace and his associates who got the treasure.

'And inside!' said Ada.

'De luxe?'

'The last word.'

'It sounds like Norton Court.'

'What's Norton Court?'

'Sir Rupert Finch's seat in Shropshire. I was butler there for a time.'

Ada squeaked emotionally.

'Are you a butler?'

'Well, I don't work at it regularly. I have private means. But I occasionally take a place. I like the work. I hope you have no prejudice against butlers?'

'I should say not. My Dad was one. Till he came into some money and retired.'

'Well, fancy that. Was this at Mallow Hall?'

'No, not at Mallow Hall.'

'Who is the butler there now? I ask because he may be a friend of mine. We form quite a close guild.'

'I heard Mr Michael call him Coleman.'

Horace shook his head.

'No, I don't know any Coleman. Who else does Mr Bond have working for him? Pretty big staff, I should imagine?'

'No, really quite small for a place that size. Just Mr Coleman and the cook and a housemaid and Ivy.'

'Who's Ivy?'

'The parlourmaid. And that's all.'

'As you say, quite a modest establishment as establishments go. Not nearly so large as Sir Rupert Finch's. But tell me more about yourself, Miss Cootes. Do you like being a secretary?'

'I love it.'

'What sort of fellow is this Mr Michael of yours?'

'Oh, he's a dear. If you go to the races a lot, you may have seen him. He's a well-known amateur rider. He rides in the Grand National.'

'Does he, indeed?'

'He came in third once.'

'Fancy that! Dangerous race, the National. I wonder his wife doesn't object.'

'Oh, he's not married.'

This was disappointing. Horace had been hoping that this Mr Michael would have had a loved wife whom he covered with jewels, these to be kept in an upper room well within the sphere of influence of Ferdie the Fly, for already the idea of obtaining the post of butler at Mallow Hall had begun to germinate in his active brain. Both Lord Wantagh and Sir Rupert Finch had been lavish with gifts of jewellery to their consorts, and it was a practice of which he thoroughly approved. Any house where there were not plenty of pearls and diamonds was of little interest to him.

And then – suddenly, as so often happened to this gifted man

– a thought came like a full-blown rose, flushing his brow. Mallow Hall had failed to meet his qualifications. But what of the bank that made mints of money? It had never occurred to him before to extend his operations to banks, but everything has to have a beginning and now that the idea had presented itself he could see that there were great possibilities in it. His acquaintance with Wellingford was of the slightest, but it had impressed him as one of those sleepy towns which are protected by drowsy police forces and jog along from day to day with no thought of crime breaking out in their midst. Why, a bank in a place like Wellingford would probably not even have a night watchman.

Sunk deep in a daydream which grew more roseate every moment, he was roused by an exclamation from his guest.

'The time!' she cried. 'I must be going. I've got to cook dinner for three.'

Horace ceased to be the business man absorbed in big business deals. He blinked once or twice and became his sociable self again.

'Dinner? Don't tell me a secretary has to cook?'

Ada giggled musically. 'How silly you are. Not for Mr Michael. I've two girls coming.'

'Rather a strain at the end of a hard day.'

'Not for me. I love to cook. I suppose it's because I'm so good at it.'

This interested Horace greatly. Cooking was one of his favourite subjects. The conversation took on a new animation as the names of exotic dishes flashed to and fro.

A sudden idea struck Ada.

'I say! Why don't you come along and join us? Or have you got to get back to London?'

'No, no hurry about that,' said Horace. 'A late train will do me all right. Thank you very much, Miss Cootes, I shall be delighted to accept your kind invitation.'

CHAPTER 3

I

Ivy, the parlourmaid, was in the kitchen feeding the Mallow Hall cats, which always dined at this hour, when she heard the back door bell ring. Going to answer it, she found herself gazing upon what the poet Tennyson would have called a gentleman of stateliest port, who beamed at her paternally and addressed her in a voice like a good sound burgundy made audible.

'Good evening,' he said.

'Good evening, sir.'

'And what might your name be, my dear?'

Ivy said her name was Ivy, and the visitor nodded approvingly.

'A very pretty name. Is Mr Coleman at home?'

'He's in his pantry, sir.'

'Take me to him, would you be so good.'

They found Coleman relaxing in an arm chair with a novel of suspense.

'A gentleman to see you, Mr Coleman,' said Ivy. She went back to the cats, and the gentleman said he wondered if he could have a word with Mr Coleman on a matter of urgency. By way of establishing cordial relations at the outset he offered him a cigar, and it was a particularly good one. Horace had his economies, but he did not practise them in the matter of smoke joy.

'My name is Appleby,' he said. 'And you are doubtless asking yourself what is the thought behind this intrusion. Briefly, Mr Coleman, I am here to put you in the way of making a bit of money.'

Eustace Coleman had accepted the cigar, but his manner made it plain that this was not to be taken to mean that he committed himself to anything. He was a wary man, and these opening words sounded to him suspiciously like life insurance. Soon, he anticipated, his visitor would whip a small book from an inside pocket and start talking about the company he represented and its benevolent practice of allowing the interest accumulating on the tontine policy to become a reserve fund with a clause permitting the accretion of both premium and interest. He said 'Ah' in a reserved sort of way, and Horace proceeded.

'But first I have bad news for you about your father.'

'My father? He died ten years ago.'

'You have your facts twisted,' said Horace, correcting him. 'He is not dead, but he is dangerously ill, and I have come to offer to take your place here while you hasten to his bedside. You are probably saying to yourself that it would be impossible for anyone to fill the place of a Coleman, but I would do my best. I may mention that I have served as butler in the best families. At the moment temporarily resting.'

A tinge of alarm disturbed Coleman. Doubts of his companion's sanity had begun to assail him. This caller appeared normal, but the novel of suspense which he was reading stressed the fact that you could not go by looks. In it the homicidal lunatic who had four murders under his belt and was contemplating a fifth was expressly described as resembling a mild University don. A quick tremor caused the ash of his cigar to drop off, and it was fortunate for his peace of mind that Horace should have lost no time in going on to explain.

'It is imperative that I establish a base at Mallow Hall, Mr Coleman. I have a suit to press. Or, as that expression is perhaps somewhat ambiguous, let me amend it by saying that I want to woo. I love, Mr Coleman.'

'You *what?*'

'And my only hope of bringing matters to a satisfactory conclusion is to be in residence at the Hall, where my loved one is employed and where I shall have the opportunity of seeing her daily and impressing my personality on her. I need scarcely tell you that the object of my affections is Ivy,' said Horace, hoping he had remembered the name correctly.

Mr Coleman's apprehensions were stilled. He had got the gist now and was able to rule out homicidal lunatics. A widower after some stormy years of matrimony, he had never had any inclination to woo Ivy himself, for he considered marriage a mug's game and would not have had a second go at it to win a substantial bet, but his eye was not dimmed and he could see that she had much to recommend her to the red-blooded male, notably a trim figure and an attractive face surmounted by a good deal of butter-coloured hair. She was also, he knew, walking out with the Wellingford sergeant of police, and he mentioned this to Horace, feeling that it was only civil to warn him of the obstacles in his path, and Horace said Yes, he was aware of that but did not allow it to discourage him. He dismissed the sergeant contemptuously as a lout.

'I anticipate little difficulty in cutting him out,' he said. 'But in order to do so I must be on the spot. Hence the little ruse which I have suggested.'

'So you want me to give my notice.'

'Precisely.'

'It should be the month by rights.'

'Not if you are called to the sick bed of a father. In those circumstances I am sure that Mr Bond would allow you to leave at once.'

'He might.'

'He would. After all, it is not as if you were leaving him permanently. His bereavement would be merely temporary – say a few weeks.'

Mr Coleman breathed out a cloud of smoke. His eyes had narrowed. There is always a moment at the conference table when eyes narrow.

'And what,' he asked, 'is there in it for me?'

Horace had expected the question.

'Ten quid?' he hazarded, and Mr Coleman smiled tolerantly, as a man will when he hears a joke that rather tickles him. 'Twenty?' Again that smile. With a pang that seemed to tie his parsimonious soul into a lover's knot Horace said 'Fifty?'

There was a spaciousness about the offer that should have impressed, but Mr Coleman greeted it with an unpleasant sneer.

'Likely!'

'What's likely?'

'You having fifty quid.'

'You think I haven't?'

'I know you haven't.'

'You do, do you?' said Horace, stung. 'Well, let me tell you I won a hundred quid at the races this afternoon and I've got it on me now.'

'Then that's what we'll make it,' said Coleman with the self-satisfied air of a man whose swift intelligence has enabled him to reach a solution agreeable to all parties. 'A hundred'll be all right.'

Too late Horace perceived that he had allowed the other's taunt to goad him into injudicious revelations. It had been madness to let a man like Eustace Coleman into the secret of his wealth. He had yielded, in short, to the temptation against which he had so often warned Ferdie the Fly and the rest of the boys, the temptation to swank and splash your money about.

It was open to him, of course, to cancel his plans and go home with his mission unaccomplished, but what Ada had said of the opulence of Bond's Bank had so inflamed him as to make it impossible for a man of spirit to do anything so weak. Besides, it would be letting the boys down, and the thought of that revolted him. True, he had not yet apprised them of the project he had in mind, so there would be no actual disappointment, but it would remain a burden on his conscience that he had had this opportunity of enriching them and had failed to take it, simply because he shrank from paying the entrance fee. Parting with a hundred pounds is always a wrench, but it would be money well spent if it enabled him to look the boys in the face when he met them.

He sighed. The party of the second part was waiting for his decision, and there was nothing to be gained by delaying it. He paid the price, and Mr Coleman tucked the money away in a back pocket.

'You wait here while I go and tell him,' he said.

'How do you explain my coming here with the news about your father?'

'I never thought of that.'

'Always think of everything. Better say I'm your cousin.'

'Or brother?'

'Cousin. I don't look enough like you to be your brother,' said Horace, who never neglected details. And, indeed, Eustace Coleman fell very short of his high standards, being meagre instead of stout and not even beginning to go bald.

When Mr Coleman returned some minutes later, it was to announce that his humane employer had made no objection to the proposed change of major domos, but had been all sympathy and understanding.

'He wants to see you, of course.'

'Of course,' said Horace. He would not have had it otherwise. The decencies must be preserved.

His opinion of Mike and Mike's opinion of him, when they met in the latter's study, were equally favourable, particularly Mike's opinion of him. The managing director of Bond's Bank might have something on his mind, but he could recognize the butler supreme when he saw him.

'I don't think Coleman told me your name.'

'Appleby, sir.'

'You're his cousin?'

'Yes, sir.'

'Well, it's very good of you to offer to help us out. I'm sorry about your uncle.'

'Very distressing, sir.'

'He's pretty bad, I gather.'

'His condition is not encouraging.'

'It's lucky that you happen to be free. Can you come at once?'

'Directly I have collected my effects, sir. They are at my residence in one of the London suburbs. And with regard to references.'

'Oh, that's all right.'

'I should prefer you to see them, sir,' said Horace austerely.

He was proud of his references and liked them to have a wide public. 'I will bring them on my return. My latest post was with Sir Rupert and Lady Finch in Shropshire. Sir Rupert was kind enough to be extremely eulogistic with regard to my services.'

'Splendid. Finch, did you say? In Shropshire?'

'Norton Court, sir. Not far from Bridgnorth.'

'Wasn't that where that big jewel robbery was?'

'It was indeed, sir, and actually during my incumbency. The view of the police was that it was the work of one of these cat burglars.'

'They're probably right.'

'I feel sure they are, sir. These miscreants think nothing of scaling the outer wall of a house. It is gratifying to reflect that Sir Rupert was fully insured. Then I will collect my impedimenta and return tomorrow.'

Horace left the room, well pleased. The thought of that lost hundred pounds was still a dagger in his bosom, but he was a practical man and knew that you cannot accumulate if you do not speculate. It was just that he wished he had not been forced to speculate to quite that extent, and he could not help thinking hard thoughts of Eustace Coleman as he started to cross the hall. He would indeed have been glad to hear that Eustace Coleman had slipped on a banana skin while hastening to the bank to deposit that hundred and sprained an ankle.

Musing thus, he was about to turn into the passage leading to the pantry which would now be his G.H.Q., where he had left his hat, when a voice, speaking from behind him with a note of surprise in it, suddenly spoke his name.

'Appleby!' said the voice.

II

It startled him not a little. Nor was his equanimity restored when, spinning on his axis, he recognized the speaker as the Miss Willard who had been on a nursing assignment at the home of Sir Rupert and Lady Finch during his residence there. The last thing he desired in his present circumstances was the society of those who had known him at Norton Court.

However, long years spent in the exercise of a testing profession had taught him to wear the mask. Giving no outward indication of inward turmoil, he said:

'Good evening, miss.'

'Fancy finding you here. You remember me, don't you?'

'Of course, miss. You were at Norton Court, nursing the dowager Lady Finch.'

'I'm now nursing Mr Bond's aunt. What brings you to Mallow Hall?'

'I am taking the place of Mr Bond's butler, Mr Coleman.'

'That's odd. I never heard that he was leaving.'

'It was very sudden. He was called away at a moment's notice.'

'And you just happened to be passing and offered your services?'

'Not quite that, miss,' said Horace with a deferential smile. 'I am Coleman's cousin. I came here to break the news to him that his father is dangerously ill. In order to enable him to hasten to the sick bed, I volunteered to substitute for him.'

Could he have done so, he would have recalled those words. Too late it occurred to him that he had entered the employment of Sir Rupert Finch owing to the sudden illness of the father of the Norton Court butler. The coincidence that he had entered the employment of Michael Bond owing to the sudden illness of the father of the Mallow Hall butler might well start a train of thought in someone of Miss Willard's intelligence.

Nor did he err in supposing this. Unlike Sir Rupert and Lady Finch, to whom he had always been in the Caesar's wife class, Jill had often wondered after the episode of the jewels if there might not have been hidden depths in this apparently blameless man. It was strange, she felt and had felt at the time, that the burglar should have known just where to look for the Finch pearls. It seemed to her that he must either have had extra-sensory perception or had been briefed by an accomplice inside the house – by, for instance, the butler. She had not made any mention of this theory, for detective work is not invited from nurses, but it had lingered with her.

And now her suspicions had leaped into new life. Like Ada Cootes and Eustace Coleman, she was fond of novels of suspense, and her wide reading had borne fruit. What she did not know of the methods of the criminal classes could have been written on a bloodstain. Horace, previously only a mild suspect, now stood revealed to her as the butler who did it, the miscreant working what is known to amateurs of novels of suspense as the inside stand. Successful at Norton Court, he was now planning to weave his subtle schemes at Mallow Hall.

'I see,' she said nonchalantly, for she too could wear the mask. 'Well, I think you will be happy here.'

'I am sure I shall, miss. Mr Bond seems a very agreeable young gentleman, and of course I know my work thoroughly.'

And if by work he meant what she thought he meant, felt Jill, he was right. Scarcely waiting for him to pass on his way, she hurried to the study. After his behaviour of the last week or so Mike did not deserve to be warned of the peril threatening his home, but she was a big-hearted girl and was prepared to overlook this, and she burst into the room all zeal and eagerness.

Mike was at the desk, deep in documents. He looked up in an absent, weary sort of way.

'Yes?' he said.

A fluid ounce of ice water flung in her face could scarcely have acted more adversely on Jill's mood of benevolence. She burned with justifiable fury. 'Yes?' he said, and in a tone that showed clearly that the mere sight of her wearied him. And this was the man who two weeks ago, if they had not been interrupted, would have asked her to marry him. If ever she had been certain of anything, it was of that. She had never lacked for what Horace would have called wooers, and the several proposals she had been compelled to refuse had all been heralded by the choky note in the voice which had been so noticeable in Mike on that occasion. Indeed, in the matter of giving an impersonation of a sufferer from laryngitis Mike had excelled all the others.

Every impulse urged her to blaze at him, as she certainly had every right to do, but better, she felt, to conduct this interview with womanly dignity. She said:

'Can you spare me a moment?'

'Yes?'

The repetition of the offensive word decided Jill. She felt that if the contents of Mallow Hall were to be removed one evening by Horace Appleby and his associates, it would serve this man right and teach him the much-needed lesson that if you go about saying 'Yes' to girls who are simply trying to help you, you do it at your own risk. So pronounced was her displeasure that she would have been perfectly capable of pointing out objects of special value to Horace and friends and helping them to pack.

'No, on second thoughts it doesn't matter,' she said.

CHAPTER 4

I

Horace's home in Croxley Road, Valley Fields, London S.E. 21 was a nice little house, though he would have preferred, and was looking forward to moving one day into, a villa on the French Riviera – a thing which of course could not be done immediately, for a man in his delicate position invites suspicion if he seems too rich. Questions are apt to be asked as to where he got all that money, and in his case such questions would not be easy to answer. So for some years now he had been living in this agreeable suburb in a semi-detached residence going by the rather frightful name of Resthaven.

Life in a London suburb can never be luxurious, but it has its advantages. A house there does not require a large staff for its maintenance. Horace employed no butler, no parlourmaid, no upper and under housemaids, just Ferdie the Fly to dust, make the beds and do the cooking. Ferdie was not as expert at cooking as at climbing up the sides of houses, but in one branch of the art he could not be rivalled. He fried a superb egg.

Two of these and the bacon that went with them were on the table before Horace on the morning after his visit to Mallow Hall, but he was not giving them the attention they deserved. He was thinking of Ada Cootes.

Normally, Horace Appleby was not much of a squire of dames these days. In his youth he had had passing romances, but grown to riper years he had put all that sort of thing behind him, concentrating solely on business. His attitude towards the other sex was, in fact, very much the same as Eustace Coleman's, in whose life since his unfortunate matrimonial experience women had meant little or nothing.

Ada, however, had made a deep impression on him, though physically, it could not be denied, she lay open to criticism. Hers, though pleasant, was definitely not the face that launched a thousand ships, and she was additionally handicapped by a square, sturdy figure suggestive of someone who in the football season turned out regularly at scrum half for the London Scottish. Nevertheless it was with a sentimental glow that he was thinking of her. Looks, he was telling himself, are not everything. Far more important are the womanly virtues for which one so often seeks in vain. These she possessed in abundance, and pre-eminent among them was her superlative cooking.

For she had in no way exaggerated when speaking of her skill in this direction. Last night's dinner had been a revelation to Horace. Not since he had served under the banner of Sir Rupert Finch, whose French chef was the talk of Shropshire, had he tasted anything so succulent. A simple meal, just steak and kidney pie with two veg and roly-poly pudding to follow, but every forkful melting in the mouth. As he furtively unbuttoned the lower buttons of his waistcoat on the previous night, he had been conscious that he was passing through a great experience.

Wandering thus down Memory Lane, he was roused from his reverie by the entrance of Ferdie the Fly. Ada's dinner party had caused him to return late, and as his man-of-all-work retired early, this was the first opportunity they had had for communication.

Ferdie was small and wizened and wore always a rather anxious look, as a man well might who so often found himself forty feet up in the air with only his natural endowments to keep him there. Life can never be unmixedly carefree for cat burglars. He greeted Horace with the affectionate respect due to masterminds.

'Morning, guv'nor.'

'Good morning, Ferdie.'

'Have a good time?'

'Excellent, thank you, Ferdie. How did you occupy yourself in my absence?'

'Basher and I went to the pictures.'

'Any good?'

'Fine. One of these spy things.'

Horace frowned. He did not share Ferdie's fondness for spy pictures. He considered spying low.

'You enjoy them, do you? Well, we all have our tastes. By the way, will you phone Basher and tell him to come here. I want to see him. Say it's urgent.'

Ferdie withdrew, to return some minutes later with the information that Basher was on his way over.

'Good,' said Horace, feeling that you could always rely on Basher. 'Well, Ferdie, what's new?'

Ferdie reflected.

'You read about Ginger Moffat?'

He was alluding to a safe blower of some distinction who after a short spell as one of Horace's boys had gone into business for himself and had had the misfortune to be apprehended with blow torch in hand and shipped off to Dartmoor.

'No, what about him?'

'He's done a bunk.'

'You don't say?'

'It was in yesterday's evenings. Got clean away. One in the eye for old Armitage.'

Horace agreed that Ginger's departure would indeed be a blow to His Honour Sir Roger Armitage, the judge who had sentenced him to five years' penal servitude. No judge likes to feel that he has simply been wasting his time. There was, of course, a brighter side, and this he pointed out.

'It is very comforting to reflect, Ferdie, that nowadays, with the security regulations so laxly observed by the prison authorities, you can always leave if the place doesn't suit you. Modern convicts can only be looked on as transients. Here today and gone tomorrow, as you might say. One no longer has that sense of bereavement when a friend is sent up for a stretch. One knows that when the fields are white with daisies, as the song beautifully puts it, he will return. I really think, Ferdie, that in these circumstances you might fry me another egg.'

This having been brought and consumed, Horace lit the after-breakfast cigar and resumed his meditations, tasting once more that flaky pie crust and those perfectly boiled potatoes steeped in their pre-eminent gravy. And presently Ferdie returned, bringing with him Llewellyn Evans.

II

He greeted Horace with his usual gentle smile. He was, as his name suggested, Welsh by birth, and his voice had the musical lilt in it which is such a feature of the voices of his countrymen.

His 'Good morning, guv'nor' sounded like the opening bars of a song hit.

'Ferdie said you wanted to see me urgent, guv'nor,' he said.

'I do, Basher, and this is my last chance, for I'm leaving this morning for the country. You'd better write down the address, Ferdie; I shall want my mail forwarded. Mallow Hall, Mallow. It's a village in Worcestershire.'

'Mallow Hall, Mallow. . . . How do you spell Worcestershire?'

'Worc is all you need. W-o-r-c.'

'Sort of hotel is it?' asked Basher.

'Big country house. I'm the new butler there.'

The significance of this was not lost on his audience. Both reacted noticeably.

'Coo, guv'nor! A job?'

'And a big one.'

'Like at Norton Court?'

'No, not this time. There won't be anything doing as regards the house. It's a bachelor establishment – no women, no jewels.'

'Then why are you going there?'

'I need a base. My objective is the local bank.'

'We're going to bust a bank?'

'Exactly. The prospect seems to pain you, Ferdie. What's wrong?'

'Nothing wrong, guv'nor, except if it's a bank, you won't want me.'

'Of course I shall want you. You will climb to an upper window and let us in.'

'That's right,' said Ferdie, brightening. 'You can't bust a bank without getting in. I didn't think of that. Do banks have upper windows?'

'This one has. It's a very old established concern. A hundred years ago I should imagine the owner slept over the office. You, too, don't look very elated, Basher. What's your objection?'

'Only thinking it can't be much of a bank, if it's in a village.'

'Relax, Basher. The trouble with you is that you're a Londoner and think in terms of Barclay's and the National Provincial. You picture a country bank as something on the lines of a pawn shop. I have made ample enquiries and I can assure you that this one is well worthy of your steel. They tell me it makes mints of money. A good country bank always does. I should imagine that Bond's, as it is called, has depositors from all over Worcestershire and Gloucestershire and Shropshire, too. Probably my late employer Sir Rupert Finch keeps an account there. And of course, it's not in Mallow Village, it's in the town of Wellingford two miles from Mallow. That dispels your qualms, I hope?'

The word was new to Basher, as so many of Horace's words were, but he gathered its import. No further beefs, he said, need be expected from him. He had a childlike faith in his leader. If the guv'nor set the seal of his approval on a job, that was sufficient for him.

'And when'll you be wanting us?'

'I shall have to let you know that later. A thing like this can't be hurried. But hold yourself in readiness to come to Wellingford the moment you hear from me. Meanwhile, have a cigar. And you, Ferdie, had better be getting about your domestic duties.'

'Okay, guv.'

Ferdie collected the debris of breakfast and withdrew, to return a moment later in apologetic mood.

'Sorry, guv'nor, I forgot to tell you. Charlie was in again yesterday just after you'd left.'

Horace started visibly.

'Charlie?'

'That's right. Didn't say what he wanted; just asked for you, and when I told him you were out, he didn't seem to believe me. He went all over the house hunting for you, and when he couldn't find you, he said to tell you he'd be looking in again.'

'Looking in again,' said Horace thoughtfully.

It was only after some moments that he was able to restore his composure with the reflection that in a short time he would be on his way to Worcestershire and that the chance of the fellow trailing him there was very remote. He was in the process of urging Basher, if he happened to run into Charlie, to keep all mention of Mallow Hall out of the conversation, when Ferdie entered to say that he was wanted on the telephone.

III

Time being money with busy business men, their tendency is always to make their talks on the telephone brief, and there was nothing in this one to cause Horace to depart from custom and linger over it. After saying 'Hullo' and listening to a short and most unpleasant speech at the other end of the wire he hung up with a nervous jerk, having had more than sufficient. Returning to Basher and sinking into a chair with every evidence of spiritual discomfort, he said in a voice far different from his usual ringing tones:

'That was Charlie!'

Basher had divined as much. Those beads of sweat on his overlord's broad brow were enough to tell the story.

'He says if I don't pay him what he claims I owe him, he'll blow my head off.'

Here Basher was able to speak a word of comfort.

'He won't do that, guv'nor. This isn't Chicago. He knows we've got a different angle on that sort of thing in England. He isn't going to risk getting a lifer by bumping you off. He'll just plug you in the leg or the arm or somewhere.'

Horace refused to look on the bright side. He had a strong objection to being plugged in the leg or arm or somewhere. He told Basher this, and Basher agreed that he had a point there. He could, he said, see Horace's side of the thing. He made another suggestion.

'Why don't you pay him his money?'

Fire flashed from Horace's eyes, which hitherto had merely bulged.

'I won't! It's a matter of principle,' he cried, and Basher saw that it would be futile to argue further. When the guv'nor took a stand on a matter of principle, there was nothing more to say.

'Well, you'll be all right once you're at that Hall place. He'll never find you there.'

Horace said he too had drawn solace from that thought. But there were obstacles in the way of the happy ending.

'How am I to get there? He said he'd be lurking outside.'

'Don't go outside.'

Horace's immediate reaction to this piece of advice was the feeling that of all the morons at present inflicting the London scene Basher was the least abundantly endowed with grey matter. Basher, it seemed to him, had an ounce less brain than a retarded rabbit. Forcing himself to a measure of calm, he said:

'If I don't go outside, how do I get to Mallow?' and Basher admitted that that was a good question. For some considerable time he sat plunged in thought.

'I know!' he cried at length.

'Know what?' said Horace, his tone indicating that it would come as a surprise to him to learn that his employee knew anything.

'I've got it,' said Basher. 'Go into the garden, nip over the fence, nip across the other gardens and carry on till you come to a road and find a bus. Charlie'll never think of you doing that. He'll be lurking out in front. And I'll bring your suitcase and meet you at Paddington.'

Horace burned with remorse and shame. Contrition flowed over him like a tidal wave. Only a moment ago he in his haste had dismissed this man's intelligence as inferior to that of a retarded rabbit, and he now saw how mistaken he had been. In the matter of brain and when it came to solving problems, no retarded rabbit could hope to compete with him. Even one with an exceptionally high I.Q. would have to acknowledge that it had met its match.

'Basher,' he cried, beaming, 'you've hit it! I'll go and pack at once.'

IV

Basher's strategy proved just as flawless as it had sounded, though to say that Horace found its execution pleasurable would be an exaggeration. Going into the garden presented no difficulties, but the same could not be said of nipping over the fences and nipping across the other gardens. It is not easy for a man of stout habit to nip over even one fence without injury to his shins, and Horace's by the time he came to journey's end were in poor shape. In one of the other gardens, moreover, he had the misfortune to encounter a hostile dog.

However, in due course he reached the road and found a bus, and arrived at Paddington in good time to catch the 12.20 express to Wellingford. Basher met him with his suitcase, as arranged, and not only met him but saw him off on the train. It was with the comfortable feeling that comes to a man who has successfully surmounted grave perils that he settled himself in his corner seat.

The compartment he had selected had only one occupant, a young man with sleek fair hair and a very small fair moustache that gave the illusion that he had been eating honey and had negligently omitted to apply the napkin to his upper lip. As Horace climbed in, he eyed him superciliously for a fleeting instant, then returned to the paper he had been reading. The train moved off, and for a while there prevailed the silence so valued by Britons on trains.

But Horace was always a friendly traveller, and this morning more than usually so, for the thought that about now Charlie Yost would be lurking in the vicinity of Resthaven, Croxley Road, Valley Fields murmuring to himself 'He cometh not' like Mariana at the moated grange, was filling him with a peace of mind that made him well disposed towards the whole human race. Alone with a member of that race, even if by the look of him not a particularly bonhomous member, he did not hesitate to embark on conversation.

'Nice day,' he said, taking advantage of the fact that the other had laid down his paper and was lighting a cigarette.

The young man turned. His eyes, Horace was surprised to see, were intelligent. Here, he felt, was a young man who thought extremely highly of himself, and against the evidence of the pink face and small moustache perhaps had some reason for his good opinion. He reminded Horace of one of his former boys, the predecessor of Ferdie the Fly, who had combined a mis-leadingly ornate appearance with a house-climbing ability not very much inferior to Ferdie's.

'What?'

'I said it was a nice day.'

'Oh?'

It was not a promising start, but Horace persevered.

'Going far?'

It seemed for a moment that the young man would signify his displeasure at this vulgar curiosity by looking cold and keeping silent, but he unbent sufficiently to utter the word 'Wellingford', and Horace, charmed by the coincidence, said that that was also his own destination.

'Oh?'

'Picturesque town. I was there at the races yesterday.'

'Oh?'

Horace decided that later on might be better for an exchange of ideas.

'I wonder if I might borrow your paper, sir?'

'Certainly.'

'Thank you. I forgot to buy one at Paddington.'

There was much to interest Horace in the morning paper, and for a considerable time silence reigned again. But it was not in him to remain silent indefinitely.

'I see they haven't caught that fellow,' he said.

'Fellow?'

'That man Moffat who escaped from prison. I take a particular interest in his case, for I was actually present at the trial.'

'So was I.'

'You are a barrister?'

'Scotland Yard.'

Horace could not repress a start. He had never before been in such close proximity with a Yard man, and he did not enjoy the experience now. No good, in his opinion, could come from mixing in such dubious company. The best he could find to say was 'Really!' in a voice so husky that, taken in conjunction with the start, it gave his companion the impression that he was overcome with awe. Gratified and flattered by a tribute which seldom came his way, for he was a very minor cog in the Scotland Yard wheel, he became unexpectedly expansive.

'Yes, I joined up when I came down from Oxford. They have begun taking in a few men from the Universities with the scientific approach, and about time. The Yard was becoming old-fashioned, fighting the crooks of today with the technique of yesterday. Badly needed new blood.'

Horace, more himself now that the first shock had passed, said he supposed so. Modern crooks, he agreed, were very clever.

'It must be an interesting life,' he said.

'It is. Though frustrating.'

'Why is that?'

'One has to deal so much with these pigheaded country police.'

'Pigheaded, are they?'

'Always think they can solve everything by themselves and never call us in till it's too late.'

'Is that why you are going to Wellingford? Have you been Called In?'

'No, I'm on leave. I was thinking of that business at Norton Court.'

Another start shook Horace's plump frame. He had to swallow before speaking.

'Norton Court?'

'In Shropshire. Sir Rupert Finch's place. They had a big jewel robbery there not long ago.'

'I believe I read about it in the papers.'

'It was nearly a week before they sent for us. Hopeless. After all that time what could we do?'

'You were there yourself?'

'I and a colleague. And I came to the conclusion that the butler – I've forgotten his name – was the man behind it. The thing stuck out a mile.'

Horace was suitably impressed.

'Quick thinking! Did you arrest him?'

'He wasn't there. He had given his notice and disappeared.'

'Very disappointing. You really think he did the robbery?'

'I don't say he did it, I said he was behind it.'

'I am afraid I do not quite understand.'

The young man smiled a patronizing smile. Horace's innocence touched him.

'It was obvious to me, though not to these yokels who call themselves police in the country, that there must have been somebody in the house working what we call the inside stand. It was his job to tell the crooks where to look. Everything pointed to the butler. I could have told in a second if I'd met the fellow.'

'You would have got him under the lights and grilled him? That is the expression, is it not?'

'I believe it is in America. We detain a suspect for questioning. But it wouldn't have been necessary. As I say, I could have told in a second. I can always tell if the man I'm talking to is a crook. It's a sort of sixth sense.'

'How very interesting,' said Horace.

In variance with his usual practice when on a train he fell

into a silence, and conversation ceased for the remainder of the journey. He was turning the situation over in his active mind, estimating to what extent the presence in Wellingford of a representative of Scotland Yard would affect his plans. He came to the conclusion that there was nothing in this new development to cause him anxiety. Why would anyone, even someone with a sixth sense, suspect the butler of a house two miles away from the town of robbing a bank in Wellingford? It was not like the Norton Court enterprise, when circumstances had compelled him to be on the scene of the crime.

His equanimity completely restored, he gave himself up to thoughts of Ada and her steak and kidney pie.

CHAPTER 5

I

With a firm shake of the head Miss Bond said it was out of the question and she had never heard anything so damned silly in her life. Just gadding about, she called it.

'I can't do without you,' she said.

'Of course you can,' said Jill. 'It's only for one night, and Ivy will look after you. She tells me she was always nursing aunts and sisters and grandmothers before she came here. You'll love having her around. Nice soft voice and a fund of good stories about the sticky ends so many of her family have come to. Draw her out about the cousin who nearly passed beyond the veil through being bitten in the leg by an angora rabbit.'

She had been asking Miss Bond, who was lying in bed with the dachshund and the two cats to keep her company as usual, for leave to go to her old home to attend the funeral of her Uncle Willie.

'And why a nice gairl like you wants to get mixed up in that sort of thing I can't imagine,' said Miss Bond. 'Were you very fond of this uncle of yours?'

'As a child I thought him wonderful. Whenever he came to our house and touched Father for a fiver, he always gave me sixpence. Later I had my doubts. He was one of those men who live by their wits and haven't quite enough wits to make a go of it.'

'A twister, eh?'

'I've heard Father call him that.'

'I know the type. Forty years ago I nearly married a man like that. Probably would have done if he hadn't gone to Australia one day without stopping to pack. Well, all right.'

'Thank you, dear Miss B. I knew I could rely on your kind heart. Shall I smooth your pillow?'

'No.'

'Mix you a cooling drink?'

'No.'

'Or take the dog for a run?'

'He can't run, he's much too fat. He's just had half my breakfast.'

'Got to keep his strength up.'

'I sometimes think he's a tapeworm cunningly disguised as a dachshund. When are you off?'

'Not till this afternoon, and I'll take the morning train back.'

'Well, mind you don't you miss it. Odd,' said Miss Bond meditatively, 'that you should come clumping in here talking of funerals. I've just been reading the Obituary column in the *Telegraph*, and I see Reggie Voules is dead. Heart attack. Aged seventy.'

'Oh, I'm sorry. Was he a friend of yours?'

'Very close at one time, and looked like coming closer.'

'Not the one who went to Australia without packing?'

'No, that was Bertie Ponsford-Yates. I nearly married Reggie forty years ago.'

'You seem to have nearly married practically everybody forty years ago.'

'They did tot up.'

'Why didn't you marry Mr Voules?'

'He lost his nerve, as so many of them did when I was a gairl. I scared them off.'

'A tough nut even then, were you?'

'I can see now where I went wrong. I couldn't keep my big mouth shut. I never learned the lesson that if you want to get your man, you mustn't be a candid critic even if it's for his own good. I was rather frank about Reggie's bridge game one night, and looking back I can see that was when he began to have second thoughts. All I said was "I know you started to learn to play bridge this morning, Reggie, but what time this morning?" but he didn't like it. After that his manner changed. A sort of wariness crept into it. He was thinking that a lifetime spent with someone who was going to say that sort of thing every night including Sundays and holidays wasn't as attractive a prospect as it had seemed. Two months later he got engaged to the dumbest gairl in Worcestershire, which is saying a good deal. And thinking of Reggie has given me an idea about you and young Mike. You say his manner has changed, like Reggie's. I believe you've been criticizing him.'

'I haven't.'

'Sure? Nothing slipped out?'

'Not a word.'

'Then that Cootes gairl and I were right. He's worried about something to do with the bank.'

'Have it your own way,' said Jill. 'And thanks again for letting me go.'

She went out and down the stairs and through the hall, and

was thus enabled to behold the new butler busy at his duties. Horace was flicking a languid feather duster over an antique chair.

'Good morning, Appleby,' said Jill coldly.

'Good morning, miss,' said Horace with the old world courtesy for which he was so justly celebrated.

II

On this, the fifth day of his sojourn at Mallow Hall, Horace was feeling, as Jill had predicted, happy and contented. There was nothing, he was telling himself, like a bachelor establishment. Chatelaines, even the best of them, are apt to get in a butler's hair, though in Horace's case one uses the expression only figuratively. Lady Finch of Norton Court, for instance, an admirable woman in many ways, had not been perfect. Interested in reincarnation, she had persisted in lending him books on the subject and he had had to read them, thus taking up valuable time when he might have been polishing his plans for the abstracting of her jewellery. At Mallow Hall he was free from such annoyances.

Musing thus, he was aware of his employer at his side.

'Oh, Appleby,' said Mike.

'Sir?' said Horace.

'I'm giving lunch tomorrow to a Mr Richards who is motoring through on his way up north. Will you tell Mrs Davis. Tell her we shall want something rather special.'

Horace looked respectfully surprised.

'Then you have not been informed, sir?'

'What about?'

'Mrs Davis unfortunately sprained her ankle this morning tripping over Thomas. One of the cats, sir. She will be unable to function for some days.'

Mike stared at him dumbly. The conviction, which had been his constant companion for the last few weeks, that Fate was making a special effort to persecute him grew stronger than ever. Tomorrow's lunch was a vitally important one. He had a favour to ask of J. B. Richards of Richards, Price and Gregory, and he had been relying on Mrs Davis to provide a meal which would put him in the mellow mood to grant it. It had been an axiom of his Uncle Hugo's that if you wanted anyone to do anything for you, a good lunch was an indispensable preliminary. One of her best efforts, he had been telling himself, would surely not fail to get the right spirit burgeoning in J. B. Richards. He had inherited her from the late Sir Hugo, who, as has been stated, was never satisfied with anything but the best, and into this category she unquestionably fell.

And instead of concentrating on dishing up a banquet which would go down in legend and song, or at least make a powerful appeal to J. B. Richards, she went about the place tripping over cats. It was the sort of thing that could happen only to a man whose luck was definitely out.

'Appleby,' said Mike, his manner, so overwrought was he, like that of a child in distress seeking aid from a wise father, 'what the devil am I going to do?'

'Put the gentleman off, sir?'

'I can't. I don't know where he is. He's on a motor tour.'

'Very vexing, sir.'

'How about Ivy?'

'Sir?'

'Could she take over?'

Horace weighed the question. The look on his face was not encouraging. He had a paternal fondness for Ivy, but remarks dropped from time to time by Mrs Davis had left him with the impression that her culinary skill was about on a par with that of Ferdie the Fly.

'Might I ask if the gentleman you are expecting is accustomed to the best?'

'I'm afraid so.'

'Then in answer to your query, sir, I fear I must state unequivocally that Ivy could not take over. Mrs Davis has been giving her cooking lessons, but I doubt if she has advanced much beyond the basic rudiments.'

'Oh, my God!'

'I appreciate your concern, sir. But if I might make a suggestion.'

A gleam of hope lightened Mike's drawn face.

'You mean you have one?'

'Yes, sir. I am in a position to state that you can find an excellent substitute for Mrs Davis in Miss Cootes.'

So dulled was Mike's mind by the bludgeonings it had been receiving of late that for a moment the name conveyed nothing to him.

'Miss Cootes?'

'Your secretary, sir.'

'Oh, *Ada*?'

'Precisely, sir. I can vouch for her virtuosity from personal experience. We met on the day you took me into your employment, and she was kind enough to invite me to dine at her residence. I am not exaggerating, sir, when I say that dinner was a revelation. She had confined her talents to a steak and kidney pie followed by roly-poly pudding, but I could read between the lines. However humble the dish, there is no mistaking a born cook. No matter how particular the gentleman you are expecting is, and I gather from what you have said that he may be described as a gourmet, I am convinced that Miss Cootes would not fail to give satisfaction.'

Mike, dazed, muttered something about always having liked Ada's buns.

'A mere side issue, sir. In my opinion she is capable of the highest flights,' said Horace, and Mike drew a long deep breath of relief. The clouds were still there, but for the first time he seemed to detect something which might be called the glimmering of a silver lining.

III

Jill came back next day, as she had promised. She arrived early in the afternoon and had scarcely washed off the stains of travel when she received a telephone call from Ada urging an immediate meeting. At four-thirty, accordingly, she was sitting at a table in the Copper Kettle, inhaling the peculiar aroma of tea, coffee, cakes, buns and customers, and waiting for Ada to join her, which she did some ten minutes later.

It was plain to Jill directly she saw her that something had occurred to stir and excite her friend. Nor did this come as a surprise, for over the telephone Ada had bubbled with an animation far different from her normal stolidity and had spoken mysteriously of momentous news to be imparted as soon as they met. Can't tell you now, she had said, because I'm speaking from the bank, and you know what it's like in a bank, Nosey Parkers in every nook and cranny listening with their ears sticking up like rabbits.

But even now she displayed an odd reluctance to tell all. She blushed. She giggled. She ate a cake with pink icing on it in a manner that could only be described as coy. But finally her secret was revealed – in a whisper, for the Copper Kettle as well as the bank had its Nosey Parkers, and one of them at an adjoining table.

'Horace has asked me to marry him,' she said, and Jill said 'What?', the whisper having been quite inaudible. At this moment, however, the Parker at the next table rose and left, and Ada repeated her words in a stronger voice.

Nothing could have delighted Jill more. She had always thought what an ideal wife Ada would make for somebody, and it had saddened her to reflect how slim was the chance of any Prince Charming riding up on his white horse in a town like Wellingford.

'Why, Ada, that's wonderful! If you're fond of him, of course.'

'Oh, I am.'

'Is he the one you were telling me about, the one you met the day of the races?'

'Yes. He says it was love at first sight.'

'Always the best kind. And you'll be Mrs what? Or Lady what? Or the Duchess of what? You never did mention his full name.'

'Didn't I?'

'If you did, I've forgotten.'

'Horace Appleby,' said Ada, and Jill's smile vanished abruptly.

'You don't mean ... you can't mean ... not the butler?' Ada stiffened. She felt that Horace's social standing had been impugned, and the implied criticism offended her.

'There's nothing wrong with butlers.'

'Of course there isn't.'

'My Dad was one.'

'I know. You told me.'

'And if you're going to say that Horace is too old...'

'No, it's not that.'

'Or too stout.'

'No, no.'

'Or too bald.'

'Of course not.'

'Then why are you being so funny?'

'I'm not being funny. At least, if I am, it's because I'm so surprised. I wasn't expecting this.'

'I wasn't expecting it myself.'

'When did it happen?'

'Yesterday. After lunch.'

'Oh, you had lunch with him?'

'Yes, at the Hall after Mr Michael and his friend had finished theirs.'

'What on earth were you doing at the Hall?'

'That was Horace.'

'What was Horace?'

'My being at the Hall. The cook sprained her ankle tripping over the cat. She had to go to bed, and this very important friend of Mr Michael expected to lunch. A big business man, Horace told me, Mr Michael had told him, who was motoring up north somewhere, and Mr Michael had asked him to stop over for lunch and he wanted to do him specially well, and no cook. He was in despair. And then Horace told him I was a wonderful cook, and he said that was wonderful and he'd ask me to come and do the lunch. So I did, and I did a very good one. And as we were eating what was left of it Horace suddenly leaned across the table and said "Ada, I love you. Will you marry me?" I was swallowing a fried potato at the time, and I nearly choked.'

She chuckled heartily at the amusing recollection, but her gaiety did not communicate itself to Jill. Jill had seldom felt less like laughing. The atmosphere of tea shoppes is always somewhat oppressive, and that of the Copper Kettle seemed now to weigh on her like a fog. In a voice which should have told Ada that approval of her romance was not universal, she said: 'Are you going to marry him?' and Ada's eyes opened in astonishment at the foolish question.

'Of course I am!'

'Did you tell him so?'

'Not exactly.'

'What do you mean, not exactly?'

'Well, I sort of thought it would be more kind of ladylike to say I would have to have time to think. But I let him kiss me,' said Ada, glowing as she relived the tender scene.

For almost the first time in her life, for she was a girl who had always known her mind and had never been slow in speaking it, Jill found herself at a loss for what to say. Ada's whole demeanour made it clear that she detected a glamour in Horace Appleby which she herself had missed and, this being so, would it not be brutal to disillusion her? She knew from her own experience what it was like to love a man and be disillusioned. And while it was hard to believe that anyone could possibly love Horace Appleby, all the evidence pointed to the fact that Ada – astoundingly – had accomplished this remarkable feat. The revelation of his true character must inevitably come as a devastating blow.

On the other hand, could she conscientiously allow her to

walk unwarned into an alliance which might quite easily be interrupted at an early stage by the arrival of Inspectors come to take the bridegroom off to Brixton or Pentonville or some other of England's houses of detention? She decided that she could not. Better for the poor girl to be disillusioned now and not after she had settled down to what she supposed would be a happy married life. But as words were still hard to find, she edged into the subject with a question:

'Did he tell you how he happened to come to the Hall? Was it to see Coleman?'

Ada shook her head. 'No, it can't have been that, because he asked me who was the butler there because it might be a friend of his, and I said I'd heard Mr Michael call him Coleman, and he said No, he had never met him. I suppose he just wanted to see the Hall, because I had been telling him how wonderful it was. And when he found Coleman was leaving, he jumped at the chance of taking his place, because it would mean being near me. A fine bit of luck finding the situation open, he said. He's always been lucky, he said. Look at the way he met me, he said. Best bit of luck that ever happened to him, he said. He says the nicest things.'

Her eyes sparkled, there was ecstasy in her voice, and Jill's resolution for a moment wavered. But her unpleasant task had to be done.

'Ada,' she said, 'can you stand a shock?'

And after that words came easily and Jill, though hating every syllable of them, did not shirk what she had to say. She pointed out how strange it was that Horace should have told her he was Coleman's cousin while telling Ada that he had never met him. She stressed the oddness of the coincidence that Horace should have established himself at Mallow Hall owing to the sudden illness of the butler's father and at Norton Court owing to the sudden illness of the father of the butler there. Significant, she said, that only a short time after his arrival at Norton Court a thief by night should have removed the famous Finch pearls, knowing exactly where to look for them. She finished by saying that a girl of Ada's intelligence could draw her own conclusions.

And it was plain from her reaction that Ada had done so. She did not speak, but she grew paler and paler as the tale proceeded. When it was done, she rose from her chair.

'I think I'll be going,' she said, and Jill was left alone, feeling like a particularly mean-souled murderess.

IV

If a keen-eyed observer had entered his pantry shortly after breakfast on the following morning, he could not have failed to notice that Horace Appleby was far from being at his spiritual peak. Ever since he had taken in the early post and read the letter addressed to him in a round female hand his brow had been sicklied o'er with the pale cast of care, his air that of a man who has received a painful blow.

A totally unforeseen blow, moreover. Admittedly Ada had said she would like time to think over his proposal, but it had never occurred to him for an instant that this was to be attributed to anything but a maidenly modesty of which he thoroughly approved. That having thought over it she would decide to reject his addresses had not struck him as a possibility. Certainly her manner when he had spoken those tender words had not been that of a girl who was planning to reject addresses. Her whole aspect had seemed to indicate that she considered the suggested union a good thing and one that should be pushed along. He had felt as he heard her musical giggle when he folded her in his embrace and kissed her that a bookie who gave odds longer than evens against the happy ending would do so only in a moment of temporary aberration. Two to one on, in his opinion, or even three to one on, would be more like it.

And now this.

She gave no reasons, she offered no explanations, she merely stated, though she put it a little differently, that having given the matter careful thought she had decided that those wedding bells would not ring out and that Horace, if he had been planning to buy new trousers for the ceremony, would do well to cancel the order.

It was not long before consternation gave way to bitterness. Several writers, notably the philosopher Schopenhauer, have said some derogatory things about the female sex, but none of them had felt more strongly on the subject of woman's defects than he did. If Schopenhauer had come into the pantry at this moment, he would have slapped him on the back and assured him that he was on the right lines.

Schopenhauer did not come into the pantry, but Ivy the parlourmaid did, with the information that a gentleman had called to see Horace, and though the last thing he desired was the society of anyone, however gentlemanly, he told her to send him in, and in due course there entered a small wizened man who looked nervous, as if just about to climb up the side of a house.

Horace stared at him, astonished.

'Ferdie,' he cried, 'what the devil are you doing here?'

'We're all here, guv'nor, all the boys. We thought we ought to be on the spot in case you wanted us immediate.'

The sight of his employee and the purport of his words had effected a change for the better in Horace's mordant mood. They reminded him that even if a woman has played him false and shattered his illusions, a man still has his work.

'Something in that,' he agreed. 'As a matter of fact I was going to phone you to be ready for action. Where are you?'

'At a pub in the town. King's Head it calls itself.'

'Who's there beside you?'

'Smithy and Frank. Basher's coming tomorrow.'

'Frank? Who's Frank?'

'Pal of Smithy's.'

'Never heard of him.'

'He's only just over in England.'

Horace started. There had been a touch of embarrassment in Ferdie's manner which struck a warning note. He looked at him keenly.

'Not another Yank?'

'Well, yes, guv'nor,' said Ferdie apologetically. 'But he's not like Charlie. He knows he mustn't carry a gun.'

'Reliable, you think?'

'Smithy says so.'

'I trust Smithy's judgment. All the same I wish these Americans would go back where they came from.'

'But when they do, think of the lolly they take out of the country.'

'That's true.'

'Bad for the trade gap.'

'Yes. Well, that's all right, then. We can go ahead.'

'Made all your plans, guv?'

'Yes, everything is arranged. You've seen the bank?'

'Took a look at it yesterday.'

'It presents no difficulties for you?'

'I could climb up it with my arm in a sling.'

'And you have the soup?'

'All we'll need.'

'Then as soon as you have removed yourself I shall take a gun from the gunroom and go out and blow a hole through one of the hall windows.'

Ferdie's brow wrinkled. He knew that any action of the guv'nor's must be for the best, but this one perplexed him. He could not see what strategic value it could have. Timidly he put his doubts into words.

'Where does that get us, guv?' he asked, and Horace smiled indulgently.

'What happens, my dear Ferdie, when I report to the police that somebody has been shooting off guns at the windows of the most important house in the neighbourhood? I'll tell you what happens. They come up to enquire, and they go away assuring the proprietor that they will watch the situation closely. And when it happens again—'

'It happens again, guv?'

'Certainly. That first shot is merely to make them take an interest. The next time, every officer on the strength comes and stands guard ... all night, I should say. And it happens to be the night when we get to work on the bank.'

'So the flatties will all be up here?'

'Precisely.'

'Coo,' said Ferdie. His emotions were similar to those of Doctor Watson when Sherlock Holmes explained his methods. He saw how foolish it had been to question this great man's most bizarre-seeming move. 'Lord love a duck,' he added.

'You approve of the idea?'

'It's what Smithy would call a typical Appleby.'

'Only what the boys expect of me.'

'That's right, guv. You're the brains, and we all know it. Your name belongs up there with Charles Peace and the rest of the really big ones.'

Horace could not restrain a modest simper.

'Oh, well, it's like the Nelson touch. One has it or one hasn't. But now, Ferdie,' said Horace, as a bell tinkled, 'I fear I must leave you. That's Mr Bond ringing from the study.'

V

Mike came out of the study as Horace reached it, and at the same moment Jill, who had been descending the stairs, stopped abruptly and stood looking down at him. Her heart, as always when she saw him unexpectedly, appeared to have suspended its functions for the time being.

'Oh, Appleby,' said Mike, 'I'm expecting the bank trustees this morning. When they come, show them into the study.'

'How shall I identify them, sir?' asked Horace in his suave way, and Mike gave the irritated little laugh of a man conscious of having said something silly.

'Yes, I'd better tell you that, hadn't I? One's General Featherstone, the other's Mr Mortlake.'

'General Featherstone and Mr Mortlake, very good, sir.'

'I ought to be back before they arrive, but if I'm not, tell them I had to go to the bank to get some papers and ask them to wait.'

'Very good, sir.'

'And put out a bottle of champagne. It's a bit early, but they'll probably need it,' said Mike with a hollow laugh as he made for the front door. And as he slammed it behind him Jill came to a sudden decision.

Ada's theory that it was some business worry that was responsible for the change in Mike had not made a great impression on Jill at the time when she advanced it, but when it was supported by Miss Bond, for whose intelligence she had considerable respect, it had gained noticeably in plausibility. Jill had been familiar with the deleterious effect of business worries on the human male ever since she had grown old enough to notice things. Anthony Willard, her father, who liked investing what money he had in strange commercial ventures, generally of the gold mine type, had always been having them, and they never failed to turn off his natural exuberance as if with a tap. He would go to bed full of good cheer, but if the morning post brought to the breakfast table a letter with bad news in it, his demeanour cast a shadow on the home for days and Jill was demoted from the position of Daddy's little playmate to that of an unwelcome stranger, stared at with glassy eyes and never spoken to except when asked if she could possibly make less noise.

And had not this – excluding a demand on his part that she make less noise – been the identical behaviour which had caused her relations with Mike so to deteriorate? Her father had looked at her glassily. Mike looked at her glassily. Her father seldom spoke to her. Mike seldom spoke to her. She was convinced now that Ada and Miss Bond were right and that it was some business worry of frightening magnitude that had removed the old lovable Mike Bond from the Mallow Hall scene and substituted in his place the depressing changeling now in residence.

Those words 'I'm expecting the bank trustees' seemed to her to tell the story. This could not be a merely social call, the objective cocktails and a chat. Bank trustees may plausibly drop in with these things in mind at five in the afternoon, but not at an hour like this. If they pay early morning calls, it means that there is serious trouble afoot.

And that parting remark of Mike's about the champagne. 'They'll probably need it', he had said, with a hollow laugh. If this was not sinister, if this did not foreshadow a crisis calculated to make the flesh creep, it was difficult to see what it did foreshadow. The writing on the wall at Belshazzar's feast had not been more ominous.

An imperious desire to be present at the forthcoming conference gripped her, and most fortunately this could quite easily be arranged. Mention has been made of a large cupboard which was one of the features of the furnishing of Sir Hugo Bond's study. Many of Jill's talks with Mike had taken place in that room, and the cupboard had not escaped her notice. It might, she now felt, have been made to her special order.

Two minutes after the front door had closed and Horace had returned to his pantry she was inside it, admirably situated for hearing all that there might be to hear and wishing that she had something more comfortable to sit on than a pile of bound volumes of some periodical presumably of interest to the landed gentry.

And ten minutes after that, though it seemed to her like a lifetime, footsteps sounded in the corridor, the door opened and Horace ushered in the visitors.

VI

Jill had never met General Sir Frederick Featherstone or his colleague Augustus Mortlake, but they were familiar to her through the obiter dicta of Miss Bond, who had drawn a particularly unflattering picture of both. According to her – she was addicted to old-world phrases – the General was a guffin and Gussie Mortlake something even lower in the intellectual scale – a gaby. The term 'footler' she applied to them equally, and why her brother Hugo had ever appointed them trustees of the bank she was frankly unable to imagine. Not wishing to boast but confident of her powers, she had told Jill that she could have made a better couple of trustees out of a piece of putty and a lump of coal.

Their conversation as they seated themselves rather bore out her critique. The General was the first to speak. He was one of those tall, lean, stringy, white-moustached ex-officers so common in the upper echelons of the army of Great Britain. In age he was approaching the seventies. His colleague Gussie Mortlake, also tall but inclining to stoutness, was in his late thirties.

'Why are you wearing riding breeches, Augustus?'

'Been riding.'

'Ah,' said the General, seeming glad that the thing had been cleared up so satisfactorily. 'I used to ride a good deal when I was younger. Not like Bond with his Grand Nationals, of course, but I once won a point-to-point.'

'I've often wondered why they call them that.'

'Have to call them something.'

'I suppose so.'

They relapsed into a meditative silence, which was broken

by the entrance of Horace, stepping cautiously to avoid spilling the bottle of champagne he was carrying on a salver. He placed it on the table and withdrew, and both trustees became simultaneously animated. It was, as Mike had indicated, early, but it can never be too early for that particular wine. The General, moreover, saw in the bottle's presence an omen.

'Champagne! That means this news young Bond has for us must be pretty good.'

'It's the only kind of news that goes with the bubbly,' Gussie agreed.

The General examined the label, and expressed gratification.

'Veuve fifty-one. Can't beat that. It was old Hugo's favourite.'

'He always had to have the best.'

'You know, a thing I've never understood,' said the General, 'is how fellows could drink champagne out of women's shoes.'

'Did they?'

'In the old days frequently.'

'Yes, now I come to think of it, I've heard that.'

'Can't have been pleasant.'

'No.'

'Still, there you are, they did it.'

'No accounting for tastes.'

'You're right.'

'Takes all sorts to make a world.'

'Exactly. Very well put.'

It is possible, though not probable, that the conversation might have plumbed even deeper depths, but at this moment Horace appeared again.

'Excuse me, gentlemen, but I thought you might be wishing me to open the wine.'

He proceeded to do so in an expert manner. Gussie looked after him as he retired once more.

'That chap's new, isn't he?'

'Took over only a few days ago, Michael was telling me. Coleman had to leave in a hurry.'

'Seems to know his job.'

'Yes, very efficient.'

'Good butlers are scarce these days.'

'Extremely.'

'Not that anyone except a plutocrat like Mike can afford one. I only run to a daily woman.'

'I, too. And she won't come on Sundays.'

'Does your missus make you wash the dishes?'

'Not wash, dry. She won't trust me to wash.'

'Life's hard, General.'

'Very hard.'

'If it wasn't for my trustee fees, I don't know how I could manage. That's why the sight of that bottle stirs me so. It must be six months since I tasted champagne. How about starting on it?'

'Before he comes?'

'Why not? It's obviously intended for us.'

'You're perfectly right, Augustus. Hugo wouldn't have expected us to delay for an instant. A great loss, old Hugo.'

'Leaves a sad gap.'

'Take him for all in all, we shall not look upon his like again, as some fellow said. So shall we... Ah, Michael. We were wondering what was keeping you.'

Mike's morale appeared to be at as low an ebb as it had been when he left the house. His 'Good morning' had the hollowest of rings.

'Sorry I'm late. I had to go to the bank to get some papers. Didn't Appleby tell you?'

'Yes, now that I recall it, he did. We were just saying what a good man he seemed to be.'

'The way he opened that champagne,' said Gussie. 'Deft, very deft.'

'Oh, he's opened it?' said Mike. 'Then why don't you . . . Oh, you have.'

'Thought we might start celebrating right away,' said Gussie. 'I always say when there's something to celebrate, lose no time in celebrating it. Well, Mike, let's have the good news.'

'I don't know that I would call it actually good, Gussie. Cutting a long story short and getting down to the salient facts, the examiners will be coming any day now to look over our books. They will find that Bond's Bank is insolvent to the tune of a hundred thousand pounds,' said Mike, and Jill fell off her pile of books with a crash that should have been plainly audible in the room outside.

CHAPTER 6

I

It was not audible, for though loud it could not compete with the extraordinary sounds that sprang simultaneously from the lips of Gussie and the General. It was as if two cats had had the misfortune to have their tails stepped on at the same moment by two particularly weighty pedestrians. They sat for an instant staring with eyes widened in speechless horror; then, as if by conditioned reflex, both reached out for the bottle of champagne. Gussie, being quicker, got to it first, filled his glass, drained it and found words.

'Is this a joke?'

Mike shook his head.

'Sorry, no. Perhaps I ought to have broken it more gently, but those are the facts.'

The General, who had been spluttering like a motor car trying to mount a hill beyond its powers, contrived to get his vocal cords into some sort of order.

'But it's impossible! It's incredible! Bond's Bank has always been like the Bank of England.'

'Till fairly recently,' said Mike.

The General fixed him with the formidable stare which had

so often struck terror into erring members of his staff. Nature had given him eyebrows of the maximum bushiness, and when he brought them into play, strong men trembled. As he bent them now on Mike, the eyes beneath them gleamed dangerously.

'Michael! Does this mean that you have been playing tricks with the bank's money?'

'Yes, I'm sorry to say.'

'Good God.'

'I was in a difficult position, and the only way out was to gamble. So, after considerable thought, that was what I did. With the unfortunate result that we are now in serious trouble.'

'We? I fail to understand you,' said the General. 'Augustus here and I are not involved in your rascally speculations.'

'Of course we're not,' said Gussie. 'I shall resign at once.'

'I, too,' said the General.

'We aren't going to get mixed up in anything.'

'Most emphatically not.'

'If you've landed yourself in the soup, it's nothing to do with us.'

'Exactly.'

Mike had not expected that this conference would be pleasant, and he was finding it fully as disagreeable as he had foreseen. He had never been particularly fond of these two trustees, who had been his uncle's appointment, but he could sympathize with their concern.

'I'm afraid,' he said, 'it's too late to talk of resigning.'

'Too late?'

'As trustees you were supposed to keep watch over the trust funds and estates in the bank's care. You found this boring and you fell into the disastrous practice of signing papers without reading them.'

There was a long silence. Both trustees were uncomfortably aware that this was precisely what they had done. Their thoughts had always been on the stipends they received rather than on the duties which were supposed to earn them.

'So you see you are quite deeply involved in what you call my rascally speculations.'

There was another long silence. Gussie was the first to break it.

'Bond,' he said, 'you are an unmitigated scoundrel.'

'I would never have thought it of you,' said the General. 'We trusted you, trusted you implicitly.'

'And all the time you were cooking the books,' said Gussie.

'It's enough to make poor old Hugo turn in his grave,' said the General.

Mike smiled a twisted smile. They had arrived at what Gussie would have called the nub.

'I doubt it,' he said. 'I don't think it would have surprised him much. You see, he was responsible for the whole trouble. I merely inherited his tangle of frauds.'

'What!'

'I can't make it plainer.'

The General appeared to be having a difficulty in breathing, and it was left to Gussie to comment on this statement.

'Are you telling us that old Hugo was an embezzler?'

'On an impressive scale. If you recall, he always did everything in a big way. When I succeeded him, I found the bank's affairs in a state you could only describe as chaotic. Uncle Hugo must have been dipping into the till for years.'

His best friends would not have called Gussie a very intelligent man, but even unintelligent men can see the obvious.

'So that's how he paid for all those hospitals and libraries!'

'That's how.'

'Well, I'll be damned!'

'We shall all be, I'm afraid. He has seen to that.'

The General overcame his bronchial difficulties, and was able to speak, though only in a low rumbling voice quite unlike his usual decisive tones.

'Old Hugo! I can't believe it. He was the most popular man in the county. We put him on a pedestal. Used to get hoarse at those dinners singing "He's a jolly good fellow". There wasn't a dry eye at his funeral. Last fellow in the world you'd have thought ... Whatever made him do it?'

'I think I can tell you that,' said Mike. 'What Gussie was saying. All those hospitals and libraries. Popularity went to his head. He was loved by everyone and wanted to stay loved, and the way to retain that universal esteem was to go on being Wellingford's Lord Bountiful. I suppose he started in a perfectly straightforward way by using his own money, and when that ran out he either had to stop being a guardian angel or use other people's. It's the sort of thing that's happening all the time. At my prep school there was a boy who was a great favourite with one and all because of the lavish way he stood treat to everyone at the school shop. "What for you, Jones?" it used to be. "And you, Smith? How about another jam sandwich, Robinson?" He didn't seem to care how much he spent. It was only later that it was discovered that for some weeks he had been helping himself right and left to the contents of his schoolmates' pockets. He, too, probably began by using his own money, and after it had gone he couldn't face the thought of having to stop being the popular hero.'

'Little beast!'

'Not at all, Gussie. He was quite a good sort. We all liked

him, even after the facts were disclosed. He's a member of parliament now.'

'He would be.'

'Yes, that must have been the way Uncle Hugo's mind worked. He ran things on a system of robbing Peter to pay Paul. Wellingford was Paul; you, General and Gussie, were two of the Peters.'

Both his hearers jerked in their chairs as if afflicted by simultaneous twinges of rheumatism. The General's hoarse voice was the first to make itself heard.

'*We* were?'

'You both had trust accounts.'

'But surely you are not saying that Hugo included us . . . his – his associates . . . his friends . . . his intimate – er – intimates in his thefts?'

'Some of those documents you found too boring to read dealt with your own money. When you signed them, you automatically became Peters in good standing.'

'Monstrous! Perfectly monstrous!'

'A ruddy nightmare,' said Gussie. 'I've been in some sticky spots before, but this one is the tops. Then the bank was insolvent when you took it on?'

'It was.'

'And you didn't say a word!'

'How could I after that funeral? The whole town had gone into mourning, everyone was telling everyone that there had never been anyone like him . . . what a noble soul . . . what a big-hearted benefactor. Did you expect me to stand up and say "You're all wrong, chaps. The man you think so highly of was a crook and a swindler"? I couldn't do it. Besides, when you're running a bank, you don't shout from the house tops that it's short two hundred thousand pounds in its funds.'

'*Two* hundred thousand?'

'That was the figure when Uncle Hugo died. Two hundred and eight thousand pounds, nineteen shillings and sixpence, to be exact. My gambles got it down to a hundred thousand, but some of them went wrong, so here we are in the unfortunate position I have sketched out for you.'

The General clutched his forehead.

'Ruin!' he said. 'Ruin!'

'Of course, there is a simple way by which the deficit can be made up,' said Mike. 'My insurance.'

Gussie started.

'Are you really insured for as much as that?'

'For that exact sum. Uncle Hugo arranged it, paid the premium for the first year and promised to go on paying it. And he would have done, no doubt, if he hadn't died. He was always generous. With other people's money, but generous.'

The General drew a deep breath.

'God bless my soul, what a relief!'

'I don't see why,' said Gussie. 'It may be years before Mike kicks the bucket.'

'Unless—'

Gussie brightened visibly.

'I think I see what you're driving at, General. You mean, of course—?'

'Exactly.'

'If he would—'

'Precisely.'

'But will he?'

'Of course he will. Out East it was an everyday occurrence. Chap got in a mess – caught cheating at cards or whatever it might be – no fuss or bother – one of us would just call on him and leave a loaded revolver – chap would take the hint and—'

'That was that?'

'Exactly. Much happier out of the whole thing.'

'Doing himself a good turn, you might say.'

'Precisely.'

Mike felt obliged to intervene in the debate. It pained him to disillusion them, but it had to be done.

'Before proceeding further, may I say that my life is insured for five thousand pounds.'

He had expected that this piece of information would cause disappointment, and it did. Gussie's jaw dropped like a tired lily, and the General had a return of his bronchial trouble.

'But you said you were insured for—'

'Just one of those little misunderstandings. I was not referring to my life insurance. The policy Uncle Hugo took out for me was slightly different. I get the money if someone injures me with intent to kill, as the legal expression is.'

'Don't be funny.'

'I'm not even trying to be. Uncle Hugo said he was doing it just in case some disgruntled depositor tried to rub me out after he had gone to heaven or wherever he expected to go. I didn't know what he meant then. I do now.'

'But you can't take out a policy like that.'

'That's what I thought when he told me, but apparently at Lloyd's you can. Lloyd's will insure you against anything. Uncle Hugo gave me half a dozen instances – the owners of a picture house who took out a policy to cover members of the audience dying of fright during the première of a horror film; a Sydney department store which insured itself against death among its customers if a Russian satellite should fall on the store; a Paris perfumer who insured against losing his sense of smell; and there were several more. Their arrangement with me is quite valid. If anyone injures me with intent to kill, I collect.'

Gussie was fingering his chin reflectively.

'It's a thought,' he said.

The General came suddenly to life.

'A damned silly thought,' he boomed disgustedly. 'You'd get ten years for doing a thing like that. And cut by the county when you came out.'

Mike continued to try to be helpful.

'No need to do it yourselves. You could club together and farm the job out to a gunman who had had a bad season. There must be some of them around who would be glad to earn an honest penny.'

'Pah!'

'What did you say, General?'

'I said Pah, Mr Bond.'

'Well, I'm afraid I've nothing else to suggest,' said Mike. 'And now, I think, as we have cleared everything up, I'll see you out. You both must be wanting a little fresh air.'

II

Jill came out of her cupboard. And it shows once again how universal is the tendency of woman to ignore inessentials and put first things first that her only feeling as she did so was one of exhilaration and relief. So that, she was telling herself, was the explanation of the chill that had crept into their relations. Not any cooling of ardour on Mike's side, not any change of heart, he had simply been preoccupied because he was ruined, as if that mattered. When Mike, having said goodbye to two of the most despondent trustees in the history of banking, returned to the study, she wasted no time in preliminary pourparlers, but flung herself into his arms with an 'Oh, Mike, Mike, Mike!' and clung to him as if they had been two survivors of a shipwreck who have found themselves safe on a desert island.

Mike's first heady feeling that something along these lines was what he had been yearning for ever since they had met lasted but a brief moment. Conscience whispered that it was all wrong, that it was precisely this sort of thing that he had been for weeks at such pains to avoid. It was heaven, of course, but a man in his deplorable position had no right to be admitted there.

'No!' he said. 'We mustn't.'

'Mike!'

'No!'

'But, Mike!'

'No!'

Jill laughed happily.

'Are you going to pretend you don't love me? Do you remember a morning when we were in here and Coleman came in to say someone had called to see you?'

'I've not forgotten.'

'Do you deny that if that fool of a butler had not butted in you were going to ask me to marry you?'

'I don't.'

'Then perhaps the trouble is that you think I don't reciprocate – if that's the word – your sentiments. Surely by this time you must have got an inkling of how I feel. Anyway, I'll put you straight on that point. Mike, will you marry me? And for goodness' sake don't blush and droop your eyes and say we can only be dear dear friends, because dear dear friends is just what we're not going to be. And don't tell me we can't get married because the bank's going to collapse. What does it matter if it does?'

Mike started with a violence almost exceeding that of his recent visitors, both of whom when he had broached this subject had started extremely violently.

'You know?'

'Of course I know. I was in the cupboard. And I'll tell you why. Because I was hoping to find out what it was that had been worrying you all this time and making you behave as if we were distant acquaintances and you were trying to increase the distance. Why couldn't you have told me? I can't believe you thought it would make any difference if I knew you were going broke. I love you because you're you, my good chump, and money doesn't enter into it. I don't care if you haven't a penny. We'll manage somehow.'

Mike's face was twisted. He spoke with difficulty.

'Jill,' he said, 'come and sit down. There's something I have to tell you. I'm afraid it's worse than not having a penny.'

'What do you mean?'

'It's no good trying to break it gently. In a few weeks I shall almost certainly be in prison.'

'Mike!' Jill's cry was almost a scream. 'You can't be!'

'I don't see what else can happen. You heard what I told those two men. About my efforts to get the bank out of its mess. Some were successful, but some failed, and it's the failures that send one to gaol. I gambled, and bankers aren't allowed to gamble with the depositors' money. If it comes off, fine. If it doesn't, it's called embezzling. I can just hear counsel for the prosecution cross-examining me, as no doubt I soon shall. "Are we to understand, then, Mr Bond, that you deliberately used money entrusted to your bank to – ah – play the market, as our American cousins would phrase it?" And all I shall have to say in my defence will be "Yes, sir, that's right, sir, but please, sir, I meant well." The jury won't even leave the box. God knows I hate having to tell you, but you can't marry a man who's going to prison.'

'I can!'

'Well, you aren't going to, my darling. I won't let you.'

For a full minute Jill was silent. Then she said in a choked voice:

'Is there no hope?'

'I can't see any. I had a big financier to lunch yesterday. I thought he might lend me enough to see me through, but he wouldn't. No, unless some kindly burglar takes it into his head to burgle the bank before the examiners arrive, I'm for it.'

Jill looked at him, perplexed.

'I don't understand. Would that help?'

'It would solve everything. If somebody broke into the bank and removed a lot of money, how would the examiners know how much had been taken? They would be nonplussed and baffled and would probably give up being examiners and go into the hay, corn and feed business. But as anything like that hasn't happened in the last hundred and forty years, it's hardly likely to happen now. I was just indulging in wishful thinking. Well, I suppose it's back to the salt mines for me,' he said, rising, 'though there doesn't seem much point in going there now. See you when I get back, my darling Jill, and try not to worry too much. I've probably been taking much too gloomy a view of things. There must be dozens of ways of getting out of this mess that I haven't thought of. One only needs to turn stones and explore avenues. And the great thing, the only thing that really matters, is that you love me. What earthly reason have I for feeling sorry for myself when I know that?'

Left alone, Jill remained where she was, staring at Sir Hugo's portrait as if musing on the problem which General Featherstone had found so perplexing. . . . Why had he done it? She heard Mike's car drive off, and long after it had gone she sat thinking. Then she went to the telephone, gave the number of the bank and asked to speak to Ada.

'Ada? Jill. I've got to see you. Can you get away?'

Ada seemed dubious.

'Well, I don't know. Mr Michael's just come in and we're doing the mail.'

'But after that?'

'I suppose I could slip out for a few minutes.'

'Then slip, my good gairl, as Miss Bond would say, and meet me at the Copper Kettle. I'll be waiting there for you.'

III

The Copper Kettle, as was pointed out earlier in this narrative, was not the ideal spot for the imparting of confidences, its popularity always filling it to capacity and its tables being wedged so close together that anyone who spoke above a whisper was to all intents and purposes broadcasting. Much of Wellingford's most interesting scandal had originated from the imprudence of clients who spoke in too carrying a voice over the coffee and cakes.

At this hour of the day, however, only a sprinkling of its patrons were present, and Jill was enabled to place the facts relating to Bond's Bank before Ada without fear of being overheard. As she did so, the thought crossed her mind that she seemed to be doing little else these days but sit in the Copper Kettle ruining her friend's happiness with bad news.

She had been prepared for a marked reaction on the latter's part as her tale unfolded, and it came as anticipated. Ada's was a stolid rather than an expressive countenance, but it was not long before it was registering amazement, shock, dismay, horror and a number of other emotions. The one emotion it did not register was incredulity. Not for an instant did it occur to her, as it had occurred to Gussie, that this revelation of the bank's insolvency might be a joke. She accepted the devastating state-ment without demur and the first thing she said, womanlike, was 'I told you so.'

'I've had a feeling for weeks there was something wrong. I knew Mr Michael was worried about something. He wouldn't have stopped saying nice things about my buns if he hadn't been. That Sir Hugo! Swanking about with his hospitals and libraries, and all the time he knew what a hole he was leaving Mr Michael and the bank and all of us in. And nothing to be done about it!'

'No, there you're wrong. There is something we can do.'

'I don't see what.'

Jill did not speak for a moment. It was not that she found any difficulty in supplying the information. It was with the object of explaining what they could do that she had arranged this meeting. What held her back was the doubt whether Ada, reeling from the shock she had just received, was in a condition to cope so soon with another. It might be better to postpone the exploding of her second bomb to a later occasion when the Cootes nervous system had had time to become adjusted to the disintegrating effects of its predecessor. A girl can take just so much in the way of shocks.

Then she reflected that there had never been anything of the weakling about Ada, of all the girls she knew the least likely to collapse beneath the most testing strain, and she decided to proceed as planned.

'Tell me, Ada,' she said, 'what happens at the bank when Mike wants something out of that big safe? Does he tell you to go and get it?'

'Unless he goes himself.'

'So you know the combination?'

'Of course.'

'Then that's all right. We can go ahead.'

'Go ahead?'

'Yes. You and I are going to burgle the bank.'

It was unfortunate that Jill should have said this just as Ada was lifting her coffee cup, for the convulsive jerk the latter gave caused its contents to spread themselves over the table and it was some time before conversation could be resumed. When a fresh cloth had been provided by a justly incensed waitress and the last apology had been made and the waitress had withdrawn with one of the frostiest looks ever seen in the Copper Kettle, Ada said:

'What did you say?'

She spoke dazedly, and Jill saw that more must be added to what had perhaps been a somewhat too bald statement of policy.

'I know you think I'm crazy,' she said, 'but when I've explained you'll see it's the only thing to be done, and you'll realize what it means to me to do it. You see, Mike and I are going to be married.'

'What!'

'Yes.'

'But you told me you didn't like him.'

'Just a slip of the tongue.'

'And you're really going to be married?'

'Yes. Or, rather, no. You see, he says the bank's done for and he's going to prison because they'll say it was his fault, so we can't get married because it wouldn't be fair on me.'

Ada seized on the operative word.

'Prison? Going to *prison?*'

'He says he's bound to unless someone burgles the bank. It's quite simple, really. If we go there and you open the safe and we take a lot of money out and hide it somewhere, the examiners won't be able to tell how much there was there originally, so of course they won't know there was a shortage and everything will be fine, because eventually all the money the bank's short of will be paid back because Mike's so clever that he only needs time. So you will co-operate, won't you, ducky? I can't make a move without you, and I know you'd do anything to help Mike.'

She could think of nothing more to say. She sat back, gazing at Ada appealingly, and her heart leaped at what she saw. Into Ada's face had come that look of stern determination which had been there when she had quelled the two inebriates with her umbrella and again when she had thrust that weapon between the legs of the predatory character who was endeavouring to steal Horace Appleby's wallet. It was the sort of look Joan of Arc might have worn when ordering her army to advance.

'When do we start?' said Ada.

CHAPTER 7

I

The morning had now reached the point where even in towns like Wellingford a good deal of activity prevails. Almost everybody was somewhere doing something, even if it was only having coffee and cakes at a tea shoppe or waiting for the pubs to open. Miss Bond was seeing her doctor. Horace was polishing silver. Ivy was getting on with some long neglected sewing. Ferdie the Fly had gone to the station to meet Basher Evans. Smithy and Frank were having a game of gin rummy. Mike and Ada were busy at the bank. And in a grubby little room in the grubby little building with the word 'Police' over its door Superintendent Jessop of the Wellingford constabulary was playing chess with his brother-in-law Sergeant Claude Potter of Scotland Yard, who was spending his leave with him.

Superintendent Jessop was extremely fond of his wife, to whom he had been happily married for many years, and on most subjects they were in complete agreement, but he was unable to share her affection for her brother Claude. It was, though he had prudently concealed the fact, with a sinking heart that he had received from her the information that Claude was to spend his vacation at their home. His brother-in-law's manner towards him, supercilious, superior and patronizing, made him ill at ease and resentful. In his presence he ceased to be the man of considerable importance in the community that he was and became what his relative by marriage not infrequently called him, a country copper.

It would not have been so bad, he sometimes felt, if Claude had been the vapid young man he looked and so could have been despised, but he was reluctantly compelled to admit that he had brains and those of a superior order. He had been the star pupil of his grammar school and had done brilliantly at Oxford, after getting a scholarship there, and while he had not yet advanced far at Scotland Yard, promotion there, he understood, was always slow. There could be no doubt that Claude was a young man with a future. And though the Superintendent disliked him, he could not deny that his conversation was interesting. He had punctuated their game with tales of life at the Yard, and the Superintendent gave a little sigh of envy.

'You've got the right job, Claude. Something doing all the time. Nothing ever happens here.'

Claude chuckled. 'Don't you be too sure.'

'What do you mean?'

'Mate,' said Claude, and the Superintendent, ruefully eyeing the board, agreed that this was so.

'You're too good for me, Claude.'

'Just a matter of using one's brain.'

'I suppose so. But what did you mean about not being too sure?'

Claude stroked his small moustache.

'Did I ever mention a man called Yost to you?'

'I don't think so. Who is he?'

'A Chicago gunman and safe blower. They cabled us from

New York that he was over here, and we had him in for questioning on a job down Wimbledon way, but there was no evidence and we had to let him go. He's in Wellingford.'

'You don't say!'

'Saw him at the pictures last night. He was in the row in front of me.'

'But what would a fellow like that be doing here?'

'Exactly what I asked myself. Then I remembered you saying what a prosperous concern the bank here was, and I realized that he must have his eye on it.'

The Superintendent gasped. A Wellingford man from birth, he had been taught to revere Bond's Bank from his earliest days. The idea of any lawbreaker, even one hailing from Chicago where ethical codes are notoriously lax, violating its sanctity deprived him of speech.

'You wouldn't think an American like Yost would have heard of it, but somebody must have told him and he decided it was worth looking into. So you aren't going to find life as quiet as you thought.'

'Are you sure he was the man you saw?'

'Certain.'

'You might have made a mistake.'

'I don't make mistakes.'

The look of care on the Superintendent's face deepened.

'They ought never to have let a man like that into the country.'

'Couldn't keep him out. His passport was in order.'

'Then they ought to deport him.'

'They probably will if he doesn't behave himself. But in the meantime be on the look out, and if he comes your way be careful, because he's known to carry a gun. Well, I'll be getting along.'

'Won't you have another game?'

'What's the use? I should only beat you. Besides, it's time I took my morning stroll. Got to give the girls a treat,' said the Sergeant, stroking his moustache.

He sauntered out, deeply sensible of his obligations to the younger female set of Wellingford, and the Superintendent fell into a reverie. He was thinking how much this brother-in-law of his afflicted his nerves and wishing that he had put his foot down more firmly when his wife had suggested inviting him into the home.

He was roused from his meditations by the ringing of the telephone.

'Yus?' he said. He had rather a bad telephone manner. 'Oh, hullow, Mr Appleby,' he added, recognizing the voice of a respected acquaintance. 'A what? . . . Somebody's shot a hole in one of your windows? . . . Good gracious. Must have given you a nasty start. And only just now I was saying that nothing ever happens in Wellingford. I'll be right up, Mr Appleby.'

II

Horace was soothing Ivy when the Superintendent arrived, for Ivy, unaccustomed to gun play except on the television screen, where there was almost too much of it, had reacted with considerable emotion to shots through the windows of houses in which she performed her parlourmaiden duties. Leaving her to go on restoring her poise with brandy, he took the visitor into the hall, his face grave, as in the circumstances was only to be expected.

'Thank you for being so prompt, Mr Jessop,' he said. 'That's the window.'

'Coo!' said the Superintendent, eyeing the damage. 'He didn't half smash it, did he. You didn't happen to get a look at the fellow?'

'Strangely enough I did. I was passing through the hall at the time. I rushed out, of course.'

'Unarmed?'

'One has to take a chance.'

'Coo!'

'I was able to catch a glimpse as he ran away. Tall, red-headed man. I could not see his face, of course, his back being turned, but I saw enough to enable me to form a theory. Do you read the papers, Mr Jessop?'

'I read the *Mirror*.'

'Then you must have read of the escape of that man Moffat from Dartmoor.'

'Yes, I saw that.'

'I am convinced that Moffat was the man who fired that shot. I happened to be present at his trial, and I noticed his height and his red hair. I don't think we need look further, Mr Jessop.'

In the matter of following Horace's reasoning the Superintendent was handicapped by a thought process as sluggish as that of Ferdie the Fly. As Ferdie had done, he gaped.

'But Dartmoor's in Devonshire. What's this Moffat doing in Worcestershire?'

'Obviously he is here for a purpose. And that purpose might have baffled me, had I not been present at his trial. You probably know that the late Sir Hugo Bond bought the Hall from Sir Roger Armitage?'

'Yes, I'd heard that.'

'But you are perhaps not aware that Sir Roger was a judge of the high court? And that it was he who presided at the trial of Moffat and sentenced him to a five-year stretch. There was an unpleasant scene at the Old Bailey when he did so. The prisoner was dragged from the dock shouting threats of what he would do to Sir Roger when he came out. And here he is, shooting holes in Sir Roger's windows, obviously with the intention of letting him know that he is on his trail. You see how the pieces of the jigsaw are falling into place, Mr Jessop.'

'But Sir Roger's not here any longer.'

'How is a man who has only just left Dartmoor to know that?'

The Superintendent was convinced. He eyed Horace reverently. Ratiocination on a scale like this, he was feeling, was worthy of his brother-in-law Claude.

'I believe you're right, Mr Appleby.'

'I know I'm right, Mr Jessop. And I feel that you should organize your men – the whole force, if necessary – and set a guard on Mallow Hall. Only if something of this sort occurs again, of course. Naturally you cannot be expected to do it every night. But if there is another shot. It may be that this one was simply a piece of bravado on Moffat's part and that he will have left the neighbourhood. Personally I don't think so. I think the man means business. His violence in court was horrifying. And unless he learns that Sir Roger no longer owns the Hall, which is most unlikely, I feel that we shall hear from him again. You agree?'

'I certainly do. One more shot, and we draw a cordon round the Hall.'

'Thank you, Mr Jessop. I knew we could rely on you. I will inform Mr Bond. And now come along with me to my pantry and we'll open a bottle of port.'

III

It was a well-pleased Horace who after refreshing the Super-intendent with a liberal libation of the late Sir Hugo's port saw him off the premises. Their conversation had had the effect of restoring his self-confidence and the faith he had always had in his star. He was a superstitious man and Ada's rejection of his suit, besides wounding his pride, had given him the uneasy feeling that his luck had at last turned. The same thing, he could not but recall, had happened to Napoleon, Jack Dempsey and others who had started out well and then struck a bad patch – so true it is that you can't win 'em all. It had shaken him. He had, indeed, virtually decided to retire from business after the conclusion of the Bond's Bank job, for after all he was so rich that he did not need to work, but the Superintendent's ready acceptance of the Moffat-Armitage theory made him feel that it would be foolish to do such a thing when he was so obviously at the summit of his form.

Such were the meditations of Horace Appleby as he sat in his pantry after his visitor's departure, and so heartening did he find them that when the telephone rang he was convinced that this must be Ada, ringing up to say she was sorry she had written those cruel words and could he ever forgive her.

It was not Ada, it was Ferdie the Fly, and a man who was feeling less complacent than was Horace might have recognized his 'Guv'nor?' as the 'Guv'nor?' of one whose soul was not at rest. Horace, however, noticed nothing.

'Ah, Ferdie,' he said. 'Has Basher arrived?'

'He's arrived, guv.'

'Capital.'

'No, guv, not so ruddy capital.'

'What do you mean, Ferdie?'

'You know what's happened to Basher?'

For the first time Horace became alarmed. Basher was the keystone on which his whole plan of campaign was based. With a quaver in his voice he said:

'He's not had another accident?'

He could not forget the occasion when a sports model car had collided with Basher in the Fulham Road. The car had suffered the worse damages of the two, but his substantial employee had had to put in at a hospital for repairs and had been unfit for business for nearly a week.

On this point Ferdie was able to reassure him.

'No, guv, not an accident.'

'Then what do you mean, something has happened to him?'

'He's retired.'

'What!'

'That's right, guv. Retired from business. Packed it up. He's gone and got religion.'

Horace gasped. The blow had been as severe as it was un-expected. From time to time, as happens to every leader of men, he had had difficulties with his little flock, but never before because one of them had got religion.

'Happened yesterday, he tells me,' said Ferdie. 'He went to one of these revival meetings. Funny thing was, he'd only gone in to get out of the rain. There was a thunderstorm round about four in the afternoon, and this revival place was handy. Afraid this rather gums up your arrangements, guv, because he says if you showed him a pete with the Crown jewels in it, he wouldn't so much as stir a finger to bust it, not if the Archbishop of Canterbury begged him on his bended knees.'

Horace was still temporarily speechless. These Welshmen,

he was thinking bitterly, you couldn't trust one of them. Take your eye off them for half a second and the next thing you knew they had sneaked round the corner and found salvation. No proper feeling, no sense of gratitude, all for their own selfish pleasures. It was only after Ferdie had twice said, 'Are you there, guv?' that he was able to utter:

'Where is he?' he asked in a choking voice.

'Having a beer in the bar. I'm phoning from the pub.'

'Tell him to come here immediately. Tell him to take a cab.'

Horace occupied the time of waiting by striding up and down the pantry thinking deleterious thoughts of the backslider, a dignified figure of righteous indignation. And in due course Basher appeared, looking larger than ever, and gave him that musical greeting of his.

It had no soothing effect on his erstwhile employer. There were two Horace Applebys – the one who breathed words of Jove into the ear of the girl he adored, giving the impression of being all sweetness and light, and the one with a face of stone, the voice of a sergeant major and an eye like Mars to threaten and command. It was the second of these who now confronted the erring Evans.

'What's all this nonsense, Basher?' he demanded abruptly, and in his voice there was no musical lilt. It was the sort of voice that might have proceeded from some particularly hard to please prophet of Old Testament days when building up a head of steam before starting to rebuke the sins of the people. A lesser man would have quailed before it, but Basher was apparently armed so strong in honesty that it passed by him like the idle wind which he respected not. His massive calm remained undisturbed.

'Nonsense, guv'nor?'

'Ferdie says you've got religion.'

'That's right, guv,' said Basher, and a stentorian 'Glory, glory' shot from him, nearly upsetting a vase containing lilies of the valley which stood on a side table. His eyes rolled ceilingwards in a sort of ecstasy.

'Yes, guv'nor, I have seen the light, and oh the peace of it. I was a lost sheep, but I heard the shepherd calling to me and I'm back in the fold and everyone's not half pleased about it. The gentleman who made the principal address said there was more joy in heaven over one sinner that repenteth than over ninety-nine I think it was he said that didn't have to, and then we all had tea and buns, and I felt cleansed, guv'nor, that's what I felt, cleansed. Glory, glory,' he added, seeming to regard the words as in the nature of a signature tune.

'Basher!' said Horace, and the vase rocked on its base again.

'Guv'nor?'

'Don't talk like a damned fool!'

A shudder passed through Basher like a shadow moving across a mountain. He pursed his lips.

'Oaths!' he said, unpursing them. 'You want to watch yourself there, guv'nor. "Swear not at all", the gentleman who made the principal address told us. Not that which goeth into the mouth defileth a man, he said, but that which cometh out of it. Don't forget, he said, you'll have to account on the last day for every ruddy word you've spoken. It's all being entered up on the charge sheet, he said.'

A forlorn feeling that he was not making progress came to Horace, but like a good General he knew how to adapt his strategy to conditions. It was plain that severity would be of no avail with this dedicated man. Persuasiveness might serve him better. When he spoke, it was with a tremolo in the voice.

'I'm shocked, Basher, shocked and pained,' he said. 'I would never have thought it. If anyone had told me that Llewellyn Evans of all men would let the side down, I'd have laughed. Laughed myself sick.'

He could scarcely have chosen a less fortunate method of approach. Basher reacted to the verb as if to a cue for which he had been waiting.

'Laugh, guv'nor? Did you say laugh? You'd laugh hearty enough if you'd see the light and lay the burden of your sins off of you, like me. You'd be as joyous as a little child. Laughing all the time I am, knowing that all those sinful acts of mine are behind me.'

That forlorn feeling grew in Horace. These were not encouraging words to hear from a right-hand man. Call them words of doom, and you would not be far wrong. But he continued to try.

'Basher, you're crazy. You can't give up a career like yours, wasting all your gifts. Think of the parable of the talents. And remember what the *Shropshire Argus* said after that Norton Court job. "The safe had evidently been opened by thoroughly expert hands", it said. It isn't everybody gets a notice like that. Mostly, the fellow who cracks a safe isn't even mentioned. And think of the boys.'

'What about the boys?'

'Their faith in you, Basher. They're trusting to you, relying on you. They're looking to you to help them clean up. They need the money.'

'The wages of sin. They're better without it.'

'I'll give you an extra cut,' said Horace, and Basher shook his head sadly.

'I was expecting this, guv'nor,' he said. 'The principal address gentleman warned me that there'd be attempts made to get at me, but he told me he knew I'd be strong and staunch and scorn the tempter. Get thou behind me, Satan, and take your extra cuts with you. If I hadn't seen the light, I'd tell you where you could stick 'em.'

Early in these exchanges emotion had caused Horace's bald head to turn pink. It was now pinker. If at this moment he had been confronted with the gentleman who made the principal address, he would not have answered for the consequences. Once again his superstitious side had come uppermost, and he was thinking that this run of bad luck he was experiencing was too consistent to be ignored. First Ada, and now Basher. It was as though Fate were warning him to watch his step.

'And what I came here for,' said Basher, resuming his remarks after thrusting a hamlike hand into his trouser pocket and bringing it out with a substantial wad of bank notes in it, 'was to restore my ill-gotten gains. I can't restore all of 'em because I've spent 'em, but here's what's left.'

And so saying, he placed the money on the table, leaving Horace revising his former pessimistic views from the bottom up. His luck, he saw, was not out, as he had supposed. Starting to count this unexpected windfall, he felt that there were compensations for the loss of Ada and that of the professional services of Basher Evans. There must be, he estimated, hundreds of pounds in this parcel of notes, and he was a man who despite his wealth could always do with additional hundreds of pounds.

It was as he occupied himself with the congenial task of ascertaining the exact total of Basher's ill-gotten gains that the door opened and Ivy appeared.

'Another gentleman to see you, Mr Appleby,' said Ivy, and Charlie Yost walked into the pantry.

CHAPTER 8

I

In the days that had passed since he had felt compelled to withhold from this labourer in the vineyard the hire of which he, the labourer, had made it so plain that he considered himself worthy, Horace had often found himself speculating as to what he would do were Charlie Yost to establish contact with him at a moment when he was alone and unprotected. At their last meeting Basher had been at his side, and his presence could always be relied on to have a tranquillizing effect on the most exasperated visitor. Just as Ada Cootes feared nothing when she had her umbrella with her, Horace could face any foe without a tremor so long as he had Basher in support.

It was now revealed to him what he would do. He would, as he had rather suspected he would, congeal in every limb like a rabbit confronted with a boa constrictor and stand staring with his lower jaw drooping to its fullest extent, fearing the worst. Watching Charlie as he advanced into the room, he was unhappily conscious that a situation had arisen to which he was unequal. He was a man of peace, his speciality brainwork, and he was painfully aware that in the encounter which threatened to develop brainwork would not serve him.

The thought that somewhere in the recesses of Charlie's neat custom-made suit there lay concealed the gun which had started all the unpleasantness would have been enough to disconcert a far braver man, for it was a gun, Horace suspected, as liberally pitted with notches as a Swiss cheese and one more, he feared, to be added almost immediately.

His relief, accordingly, when his visitor opened the proceedings with a cheery 'Hi', was stupendous. Its friendly ring seemed to suggest that bygones were to be considered bygones and all their little differences forgotten and forgiven. Getting his vocal cords into some sort of order, he replied with a 'Hullo, Charlie' as effusive as he could make it. The words came out with more of a croak than he could have wished, but they seemed to have been well received, for Charlie's affability continued undiminished.

'Wondering how I tracked you down?' he said. 'I ran into a guy called Frank I used to know on the other side, and he told me where you were. Nice place you've got here.'

Horace agreed that Mallow Hall had many merits.

'There's nothing to beat these old English country houses,' said Charlie, becoming lyrical. 'All those parks and gardens and terraces and stuff. Makes you think of bygone ages and knights in armour and all like that. I saw one of these joints in a movie in Cicero once with Fred Astaire in it, and I remember thinking those guys have it pretty soft. Who does this place belong to?'

'Mr Michael Bond. His uncle, the late Sir Hugo Bond, bought it from Sir Roger Armitage, whose family had lived here for several centuries. Sir Roger is a Judge of the High Court.'

'One of those, eh? Rich?'

'I believe he has a good deal of money.'

'Probably made it taking bribes. And while we're talking of money,' said Charlie Yost, giving a clue to his unexpected geniality, 'I see you've got mine all ready for me. That's what I call service.'

And before Horace's shocked eyes he sauntered to the table and scooped up and trousered its contents.

Horace did his best.

'You can't take that, Charlie. It's Basher's.'

'Not now,' said Charlie Yost.

Silence fell. It was scarcely to be expected that after the incident just recorded the atmosphere of harmony and good will in which this interview had begun would continue unimpaired, and an acute observer would have noticed, on Horace's part at least, a certain strain, as if like the poet Wordsworth when he saw a flower, he was experiencing thoughts too deep for tears. He should have been consoling himself with the reflection that Charlie with his persuasive methods would in any case have extracted money from him and how much better that it should be money donated by Basher rather than his own personal cash, but he was not. All he was thinking was how agreeable it would be to take up the decanter of port which stood on the table and bring it down with a solid thump on Charlie's head. This not being within the sphere of practical politics, for how would one manage all that business of getting rid of the body, he merely sat and glowered, leaving the cheerfulness to his companion.

Fortunately for the success of the party Charlie had cheerfulness enough for two. He was feeling happy and relaxed. He had come expecting a difficult business talk, possibly even a vulgar brawl, and it was a relief to have found the interview turning into a purely social one – just two old cronies getting together and chatting over a glass of whatever it was that was in that decanter.

'What is it?' he asked, and Horace replied sourly that it was port, and Charlie, who had never tasted port, welcomed this opportunity of filling the gap in his education. He reached out for the decanter and took a hearty draft. This proving most enjoyable, he took another.

'This is good,' he said. 'Sort of a soft drink, isn't it?'

Horace shuddered. This blasphemy, coming so soon after his monetary loss, seemed to him more than a man could be expected to endure. He replied stiffly that it was not.

'Its alcoholic content is quite pronounced.'

'Well, that's how we like alcoholic contents to be, don't we?' said Charlie sunnily. He drank deeply once more, and Horace averted his eyes. Even before the gun episode he had never been fond of Charlie, and the uncouth way in which he was gulping the precious fluid rather than sipping it reverently increased his dislike. 'Yes, I'd say it was pronounced all right. Quite a kick. What did you say it's called?'

'Port.'

'Do you suppose they'd have it over in Chicago?'

'I imagine port of a sort might be obtained there.'

'I must get some. You've never been in America, have you?'

'No.'

'You ought to go,' said Charlie. 'Yes, sir, you certainly ought to go. That's the place. God's country. Not that I've anything against England, but it's not the same. You know what I miss over here? Our cops. Yours don't provide the same excitement. Too polite. I was pulled in for questioning the other day at that Scotland Yard place and there was no *tang* about it, no zip, none of that sense of living dangerously you have on our side when they get you into the interrogation room and turn on the lights. You'd have thought they didn't want to hurt your feelings. Yes, sir, you certainly ought to go to the States. You'd do well there. So would Ferdie. Basher I'm not so sure about. Too much on the dumb side. By the way, how come you say that money was Basher's money? Didn't seem to me to make sense.'

'He was here just before you arrived. He left it on the table.'

After imbibing so much of the port with its pronounced alcoholic content Charlie's brain was not at its keenest. He found the explanation inadequate.

'Basher did?'

'Yes.'

'Left it on the table?'

'Yes.'

'You mean he forgot it?'

'No, he gave it to me.'

'*Gave* it to you?'

'Yes.'

'He must be nuts.'

'He is,' said Horace bitterly. 'He called that money the wages of sin and said he wanted to get rid of it. Basher's gone and got religion.'

'You're kidding.'

'No. He sneaked off to one of those revival meetings and they converted him, curse him.'

It would have been more tactful of Charlie Yost, for he could see that his former employer was greatly moved, not to have laughed at this piece of information; but his dealings with the decanter had left him in a frame of mind when almost anything would have seemed hilarious to him, and the rich comedy of someone like Basher getting religion was irresistible. He guffawed as heartily as a studio audience, and Horace eyed him sourly.

'Think it's funny, do you? Well, I don't. It only ruins all my plans, that's all it does.'

Charlie was still chuckling softly as he polished the lenses of his spectacles, which the tears of mirth had dimmed. At these words he looked up sharply.

'What plans? You got a job on?'

'Yes.'

'And you needed Basher?'

'Yes.'

'Something to do with safes?'

'Yes.'

'Then why don't you let me in on it? I'm at liberty and anything Basher can do I can do better.'

Horace started. The suggestion had come as a complete surprise to him, and like all new ideas it took some assimilating. Nothing at the beginning of this conversation could have been further from his mind than the thought of resuming relations with a man who had not only deprived him of a large sum of money but who gulped Sir Hugo's priceless port as if it had been the rye or bourbon of his native land. He had talked with him; in the matter of the port he might be said to have been his host; but the last thing he would have contemplated was the taking him on again as one of his boys. Where Charlie was concerned, he would have said that he had had it. All he had felt as far as their future association was involved was that he would take the high road and Charlie the low road and it was his fervent hope that he would never set eyes on the man again.

But the defection of Basher altered everything. It had left

him in no position to indulge private animosities. A sensible man, he realized that what Operation Bond's Bank required was not a safeblower for whom he entertained a warm personal regard but one good at blowing safes, and in this respect Charlie's qualifications were undeniable. He was honest enough with himself to admit that he would never have given Basher the assignment if Charlie Yost had been available. So now it was for only a brief moment that he hesitated, and when Charlie said 'How about it?' and urged him to think on his feet, he replied that he found the proposition quite acceptable. There was no ring of affection in his voice as he said it, but his guest was far too full of port to notice its absence.

'It's a deal, then,' said Charlie. 'And this time,' he added in rather a marked manner, 'no funny business. Well, see you on the barricades,' he said, and took his leave.

Emerging into the gardens of Mallow Hall with a song on his lips, the first thing he saw was Basher, bent over a rose bush. He had missed him on his arrival, for that flower-loving man had wandered off to examine some sweet peas behind a distant pergola. Basher, who lived in Brixton, which does not go in much for floral displays, was deriving considerable spiritual uplift from the handiwork of the late Sir Hugo's gardening staff. His first intimation that he was not alone with Nature came when Charlie slapped him genially on his spacious trouser seat. Straightening himself up, he regarded him with surprise.

'Why, Charlie! What in the world are you doing here?'

'Came to see the boss.'

'Me, too. I was in with him just now.'

'So he told me.'

'Had to bring him some bad news.'

'He told me that, too. Got religion, haven't you?'

'Yes, I'm saved, Charlie. I'm what they call a brand from the burning.'

'Good for you. But not so good for him. He said you wanted out from this bank caper and it left him in a spot.'

'I did what my conscience bade me. I rejoice to think that I have stopped him doing that sinful thing.'

'But you haven't, pal. I'm pinch hitting for you.'

'What!'

'Sure. It's all settled. We're buddies again and I'm back on the pay roll.'

A look of concern spread itself over the vast expanse of Basher's face.

'I wouldn't, Charlie. Look in your heart and ask it if you're doing right.'

'I did, and it said I couldn't do better. Go to it, it said.'

Basher's concern deepened.

'You won't half cop it on Judgment Day, Charlie.'

'Who says so?'

'The gentleman who made the principal address at the meeting where I got saved. He said I would have done if I'd carried on in my old way. He said I'd repented only just in time. Another couple of jobs, he said, and I'd have been for it. You ever been in a bakery, Charlie?'

'Not that I remember.'

'Go to one and take a look at the fire they've got there. Flames that burn and scorch. But nothing to what's waiting for you if you go busting banks. Where are you staying, Charlie?'

'A dump called the Blue Lion on Main Street.'

'I'll come and see you tonight and wrestle with you in prayer.'

'Sure,' said Charlie Yost amiably. 'Any time you're passing.'

He went on his way with a cheery 'Be seeing you', and was soon passing through the great gates that opened on the high road. And he had walked – a little unsteadily but feeling extraordinarily well and happy – for perhaps half a mile, when he perceived coming out from the smaller gates of a house just visible through a belt of trees a man in riding breeches who paced slowly, as if he were not in the best of spirits.

11

After leaving Mike, Gussie Mortlake had accompanied General Featherstone to the latter's house for a discussion of the situation, and he was now on his way to his own residence, where he proposed to give the crisis further intensive thought over a whisky-and-soda as strong as hand could make it. He did not as a rule drink in the morning, though, as we have seen, glad of a glass of champagne if he could get it, but a man beneath whose feet a large bomb has recently been exploded may be excused for deviating from his normal habits. Gussie was looking forward to that whisky-and-soda as harts are said to do for cooling streams when heated in the chase.

The day was calm and sunny, in which respect it differed radically from this victim of the late Sir Hugo's financial eccentricities. As he came out on to the high road he was thinking unkind thoughts of the late Sir Hugo and bitterly regretting the fifty shillings he could ill spare which he had squandered on a wreath for the other's funeral. He was also feeling not too friendly towards General Featherstone, who had continued to heap scorn on Mike's suggestion that they should dispose of all their difficulties by hiring a gunman to shoot him with intent to kill. It seemed to Gussie a most admirable suggestion, one that would solve everything.

Of course there was the problem of where to find the gunman, and he could see that this called for some thought. In the United States of America, he understood, the traffic in these fauna was brisk, and all you had to do if you wanted one was to put an advertisement in the paper or skim through the yellow pages of the telephone directory, but this was England, where such a procedure presented difficulties. Nevertheless, he was convinced that a little research would produce results, and so sure was he of this that when at this moment Charlie Yost suddenly thrust the muzzle of a pistol against his abdomen with the words 'This is a stick-up', his immediate thought was that here was the very desperado he had been planning to scour the country for. As so often happens, the hour had produced the man.

It was that port of Horace's which had put into Charlie's mind the whimsical idea of sticking Gussie up. Just for kicks, of course. There was no thought of sordid gain in his mind. As a young fellow breaking into the game he had frequently done this sort of thing for profit, but those days were far distant. Risen to his present prominence in safe-blowing circles, he had long since abandoned a practice so beneath the dignity of a substantial citizen. But the port had left him lighthearted and in the mood for a nostalgic return to the follies of his youth. So he prodded Gussie as described, and there for a moment the matter rested. Gussie, who had seen enough gangster pictures to know the drill on these occasions, had reached for the sky, as he believed the technical expression was, while Charlie, now that he had time to think, was beginning to ask himself if he had not allowed nostalgia to lead him into a course of action which he would subsequently regret. And at this moment round the corner on his bicycle came riding Sergeant Herbert Brewster of the Wellingford police.

Reference has already been made to the fact that a state of something deeper and warmer than ordinary friendship existed between this Sergeant and Ivy, the Mallow Hall parlourmaid. They had been walking out for some months, and it was the Sergeant's habit, when his bicycling took him near the Hall, to look in and have a cup of coffee and a chat with Ivy in the kitchen. He had done so today and was returning to his base, when ahead of him on the high road his eye was caught by the sight of a small man in horn-rimmed spectacles and a taller man in riding breeches, in whom he recognized Mr Mortlake, a fellow member of the Wellingford cricket team. And Mr Mortlake was standing with his hands extended skywards.

A patron, like Gussie, of the pictures, Sergeant Brewster did not need to be told what this meant. Incredible as it might seem in the heart of peaceful Worcestershire, he was witnessing a stick-up, and had he been a more sensitive man, he might have felt a pang of pity for a criminal so optimistic as to hope to reap financial profit from sticking up Augustus Mortlake. But his only thought was that here was a heaven-sent opportunity of making a cop which would hardly fail to advance his professional career. His eyes gleamed, he pedalled swiftly to the scene of the crime, and Charlie Yost, observing his approach, felt that the doubts he had entertained concerning the wisdom of the course he had pursued had been well founded.

Policemen being men of action rather than of words, many of them on occasions like this find themselves at a loss for a suitable opening speech and have to fall back on the official 'Ho', but Sergeant Brewster experienced no such embarrassment. In a stern voice which had the worst effect on Charlie's morale, he said:

'What's all this?

'Having a little trouble, Mr Mortlake?' he added, and Charlie waited apprehensively for Gussie's reply.

He might well have felt apprehensive. Horace, when rebuking him for carrying a gun during business hours, had been at pains to explain how dim was the view taken of this practice by the law of Great Britain, and his words came back to Charlie now with sickening clearness. In England, Horace had seemed to suggest, you could do practically what you liked in the way of crime provided there were no firearms on your person, but if you were caught with anything in the nature of an arsenal in your possession, you did not have to wait till Judgment Day to get what was coming to you.

Charlie, who always felt nude without a gun on him, had been unimpressed and defiant at the time, but now his emotions were very different. He shrank beneath Sergeant Brewster's accusing eye. A palmist had once told him that one of these days a dark man would cross his path and that from this dark man a good deal of unpleasantness was to be expected. In the Sergeant, whose swarthy face justified that description, he felt that he had found him.

Gussie was lowering his arms.

'Oh, hullo, Herbert,' he said. 'Trouble? No, no trouble, thanks. This gentleman was asking me for a match.'

'You were holding up your hands.'

'Just stretching. Touch of cramp.'

'It wasn't a stick-up?'

'Good heavens, no. What an extraordinary idea.'

'Ho!' said the Sergeant.

It was, of course, what he ought to have said at the beginning, and he said it now in a voice rendered unmusical by chagrin and frustration. Nothing so saddens a police sergeant as to have his dreams shattered just when everything had seemed to be going so well. Sombrely he mounted his bicycle, and with bowed head pedalled off. If ever in the whole history of England's police procedure a sergeant of police had drained the bitter cup and bicycled with vultures gnawing at his bosom, this sergeant of police was that sergeant of police.

But it often happens that when one man – call him A – is in the depths and brooding darkly on what might have been, another – call him B – is feeling fine. It was so on the present occasion. To Charlie Yost the sun seemed to be shining with exceptional resplendence, and the singing of the birds had taken on a sweetness and purity unusual even in Worcestershire, where the birds are always in good voice. And what had led to this improvement in local conditions had been the astounding forbearance of Augustus Mortlake. He gaped at him, overcome. He had never dreamed that any man in riding breeches could be so noble.

'Say!' he said when he was able to speak. 'That was swell of you.'

Gussie waved away the tribute, his air that of a man who wants no thanks.

'Don't mention it. Only too pleased.'

'I wish there was something I could do for you.'

'There is.'

The light of devotion gleamed from Charlie's spectacles. His voice trembled.

'You name it, I'll do it.'

'It's a bit complicated. I ought to warn you that it'll take some time to give you a thorough grasp of the gist.'

'My time's yours.'

'Well, it's like this,' said Gussie.

III

At the bank Mike was sitting in his private office dictating letters to Ada Cootes, when he was informed that Mr Mortlake had called to see him.

Even in the most favourable circumstances he was seldom anxious to talk to Gussie and after their recent conference he felt that he would find his company more than ordinarily oppressive. The best you could say of him was that he was not General Featherstone. However, a bank manager cannot deny himself to visitors, and a moment later Gussie entered, surprisingly accompanied by a small man in horn-rimmed spectacles who looked as if he might be an out-of-work clerk come to apply for a job. It seemed to Mike that this small man had a pensive air, as if he were meditating on something.

And, indeed, this was just what Charlie Yost was doing. Passing through the bank he had of course noticed the great safe which was one of its features, and its solidity had impressed him. It was, he could see at a glance, the sort of safe which would take a full measure of blowing, and he was not at all sure that he was equal to its demands. But with your true professional these moods of self-distrust never last long. He recalled previous triumphs against similar odds and was able to cast off misgivings and summon up a smile as Gussie performed the introductions.

'This is Mr Yost, Mike.'

'How do you do?' said Mike, by a hairsbreadth avoiding the solecism of saying 'Mr *What*?'

'Mr Bond, Charlie.'

'Pleased to meet you, Mr Bond. Nice day.'

'Very.'

'We've come to see you,' said Gussie, 'on an important matter.'

'Oh, yes?'

'A *private* important matter.'

'Oh? Would you mind, Ada?'

'Certainly, Mr Michael.'

Ada withdrew and Charlie put a question.

'This joint isn't bugged, is it?'

'Bugged?'

'There aren't any microphones he means,' Gussie interpreted. 'Because if there are, we'll have to keep our lips sealed and hold this summit meeting in the cellar or somewhere.'

'I see. No, no microphones,' said Mike, feeling that, unless it was just his imagination, Gussie was being more of an ass even than usual. 'I'm rather busy,' he added, thinking that it was time a hint was dropped, and Gussie said 'Of course, of course, of course.'

'Too bad muscling in like this, but it had to be done, and you'll find, when you've heard all, that what we've come to say hasn't wasted your time. I want you, Mike, to throw your mind back to that conversation you and I and the General had this morning. I've been telling Mr Yost about it. Oh, not the early part,' Gussie, seeing his quick look of concern, hastened to assure him, 'just what you said towards the end. You remember what you said towards the end? The talk had turned to your urgent need of collecting a bit of money quick, and you told us you were insured for a substantial sum against getting injured with intent to kill, so if somebody injured you with intent to kill, you'd be sitting on top of the world. You've not forgotten?'

Mike said it had not slipped his memory.

'The General,' Gussie continued, 'didn't think much of the idea, if you recall, but you've always got to budget for that sort of hidebound attitude in military men, especially when well stricken in years and on the retired list. I thought it fine. It would solve all our – I mean your problems in a flash. But there was a snag, the difficulty of finding someone to do it. Fellows who go about injuring chaps with intent to kill don't grow on trees. However, most fortunately, I happened to run into Mr Yost, who has been in that line of business for years, and he says he'll be charmed to plug you any time you name and won't charge you a cent. Beat that for a stroke of luck,' said Gussie.

It was with mixed feelings that Mike turned his attention to this big-hearted benefactor. One of these feelings was surprise. Nothing in Charlie's aspect suggested that he would be capable of injuring even a mosquito with intent to kill, and he was experiencing some difficulty in absorbing the revelation of this unsuspected side to his character.

He was also conscious of what Horace would have called qualms, for however much it may benefit a man to be plugged, it is never easy for him to enjoy the prospect. Nor did the fact that the scheme which Gussie had sketched out had been his own idea seem to make it any better.

'Plug me?' he said. 'Plug me where?'

'Well, in your home would be the best place,' said Charlie, suddenly becoming vocal. 'You see, you got to make the thing look natural on account that when you nick these insurance people for anything kind of big, they're apt to ask questions. Take for instance you walk in on them with your arm in a sling and say "Lookut. See what a guy just done to me out on the street." They say "Who was he?" "Search me. I don't know," you say. "Enemy of yours?" they say. "I tell you I never saw the character before in my life," you say. "I was walking along, minding my own business, when he outed a gun, upped with it and started throwing lead around." "Then how do you know he was shooting with intent to kill?" they say. "Probably just an accident. His hand slipped." And there you are with an expensive law suit on your hands. The only guy that can plug you and make it look natural is a burglar, on account that if a burglar's in a jam and sees a pinch coming, nine times out of ten he'll try to shoot himself out of it. Here's the set-up as I see it. We fix the night and I bust into your home. You catch me, and I let you have it. That way there's no unpleasantness. Sort of thing that's happening all the time. Nobody'll say a word.'

'I see. But when I asked where I was to be plugged, I meant in what particular portion of my anatomy.'

'Ah, I get you. Why, anywhere, anywhere,' said Charlie with an airiness which struck Mike as out of keeping with the gravity of the situation. 'Leg, arm, shoulder, anywhere you think best. You name it, I'll plug it.'

It seemed to Gussie, watching him anxiously, that Mike was showing a disturbing lack of enthusiasm. The thought occurred to him that he had not worked the thing out from every angle and thus had failed to realize how vital to the well-being of one and all was the co-operation of this obliging gunman. This must be done at once, and as it could hardly be done in the presence of Charlie, he now asked the latter to leave them.

'Frightfully sorry, but there's something extremely private I have to confer with Mr Bond about.'

'Sure,' said Charlie amiably. 'Pleased to have met you,

Mr Bond. You'll find me at a dump on Main Street called the Blue Lion, if you want me.'

'Oh, we'll want you all right,' said Gussie.

He was confident that the eloquence he was proposing to pour forth on Mike could not fail to get him thinking along the right lines.

The gaze he directed at him as the door closed was stern and rebuking.

'What's the matter with you, Mike?' he demanded.

Mike stirred from the reverie into which he had fallen.

'Matter?'

'Yes, matter. When I brought Mr Yost in and revealed how he was going to extract us from the soup, I was expecting you, if not to skip like the high hills, at least to let your eyes sparkle a bit as you contemplated the good fortune which had befallen us. It isn't every gunman who'd be willing to take on a job like this for nothing, and you might at least have given him a word of thanks for his extremely sporting offer. Instead of which, you just sat there and looked at him as if he were something the cat had brought in.'

'Well, he isn't much to look at.'

'That's not the point. I grant you that he would never get far in a male beauty contest, but, good Lord, when you want a man to plug you, what does it matter if he isn't a sort of matinee idol? The only question you have to ask yourself is, Is he a good shot?'

'And is he?'

'Of course he is. He's a prominent Chicago gunman. He's been shooting people all his life, and I cannot advise you too strongly to place yourself unreservedly in his hands. Nothing but good can result from it, and it won't hurt, if that's what's bothering you. No worse than a bad cold.'

'Who says so?'

'Everybody says so. You must have read about fellows who get shot. They don't feel a thing. It's only after half an hour or so that they notice there's anything wrong. "Bless my soul," they say. "I seem to have got a hole in me. Now how did that happen?" Charlie tells me he's been perforated oftener than a social security cheque and never noticed it. You really must stop making these frivolous objections, Mike. Try to realize how this is going to get us all out of the red. Put your trust in Charlie Yost and the bank won't bust, and you and I and the General won't go to chokey, and everything will be fine. Whereas if you don't, we'll all be eating skilly, whatever that is, and sewing mail bags. Don't be a chump, Mike. Grasp an opportunity which won't occur again.'

He had not overestimated the power of his eloquence. It would be exaggerating to say that Mike brightened, but he attempted no counter argument.

'All right,' he said.

'You'll co-operate with Charlie?'

'It seems to be the only way.'

'It is. Let's go.'

'Go where?'

'To the Blue Lion,' said Gussie.

CHAPTER 9

I

Night had fallen on Wellingford with the thoroughness with which night always falls on that type of town. Its shops were shut, its streets empty, its two motion picture houses long since barred and shuttered. Only in Bond's Bank did life continue to function. It had closed, of course, many hours earlier, but unlike the shops and the cinemas it was still occupied. In its main office Jill was standing with Ada in the pitch darkness which comes to banks when the hour is late and the lights have been turned off.

Although Jill could not see Ada, it comforted her to know that she was there, for the natural trepidation which a girl feels when burgling for the first time had been greatly increased by the fact that a good many ghosts seemed to have got into the place. They were not squeaking and gibbering as had happened in Rome a little ere the mightiest Julius fell, but she could sense their presence and they were hostile ghosts, ghosts of bygone Bonds, Bonds of Regency days in tight trousers and stiff cravats, Victorian Bonds with top hats and flowing whiskers, all justifiably resenting this intrusion on their sacred premises. The thought crossed Jill's mind that if the spectre of the late Sir

Hugo had accompanied them, it was like his nerve, for but for him the intrusion would not have been necessary.

She clenched her hands and drew a deep breath.

'Out of the night that covers me, black as the pit from pole to pole, I thank whatever gods may be for my unconquerable soul,' she said, and Ada said, 'What?'

'Just encouraging myself, chum. It's a tip I got from my Uncle Willie when I was a kid. He said he always recited those lines to buck him up in times of crisis, and what he didn't know about times of crisis wasn't worth knowing. He was the black sheep of the family, always a jump ahead of total ruin, and whenever he dropped in on us Father used to feel like the Lady of Shalott, knowing that the curse had come upon him and a loan of at least a fiver was inevitable. And fivers were never plentiful round our way.'

'Who was the Lady of Shalott?' Ada asked, and Jill said, 'Oh, it's a long story. I'll tell you some other time. You have probably gathered from the way I'm babbling,' she said, 'that I'm scared stiff. How are conditions at your end?'

'I'm all right,' said Ada, whom very few things were able to disturb. 'It's only it all being so dark that's making you jumpy. I'll switch the light on.'

'Dare we? Is it safe?'

'Well, we've got to do it some time,' said Ada in her practical way, 'or how can we see? Anyway, the shutters are closed. There.'

The lights flashed on, and immediately Jill felt better. It was not often that she gave way, even for a moment, to girlish tremors.

'Now we're off,' she said. 'But there's still something that's worrying me a little. We're hoping everyone will assume that this job has been done by professionals, but will they?'

'Why not?'

'How did they get the safe open? They didn't just unlock it, did they?'

'Yes, they did. They found the combination.'

'How?'

'It's in Mr Michael's notebook. He keeps it in that little safe over there. He was always forgetting it, so I made him write it down. They just hunted around and there it was. We'll leave the safe open when we go.'

'I see. Yes, that seems plausible enough. But it's a pity we're poor weak females who can't use the proper burgling tools which would have made the thing really convincing. Still, looking on the bright side, think how tiring it would have been. I suppose that's the drawback to the burglar's life, the hard work. What's the matter?'

'Nothing.'

'You heaved a sigh.'

'I didn't mean to.'

'But you did.'

'Oh, well, if you really want to know, I was thinking of Horace.'

'I thought so!'

'It makes me so miserable to feel that this is the sort of thing he does.'

'Actually, it isn't. Mr Appleby takes no part in the practical end of the work. He's the mastermind in the background, the spider sitting in its web and weaving its schemes. I don't suppose he's ever used a jemmy or a centrebit in his life.'

'It comes to the same thing. Oh, dear!'

'Buck up, old thing.'

'I can't.'

'You really love him?'

'Oh, I do.'

'Oh, Ada, I wish you didn't. I was hoping you'd have been getting over it.'

'I'll never get over it.'

Once again the miracle of anyone being able to love Horace Appleby held Jill speechless. And she found herself regretting that she had opened Ada's eyes to his true character and had not let her take her chance of whatever marriage with him might bring. After all, many men with the shakiest ethical codes had made good husbands.

She, too, sighed.

'We're not very lucky in our choice of mates, are we, Ada? You won't marry your man because you don't approve of his way of making a living, and the only man I ever wanted to marry has the shadow of prison hanging over him. And the tragic part of it is that I'm a one-man girl. If I can't have Mike, I don't want anyone. I'll settle down as an old maid and keep cats.'

'Can they really send Mr Michael to prison?'

'He says they can and I suppose he knows. It's a damned shame he should be in a jam like this. He never wanted to come into the bank. He'd have liked to emigrate to America or Canada or somewhere and got some job that would keep him in the open air, but Sir Hugo persuaded him that it was his duty to carry on the family tradition, and look where it's landed him. You know, Ada, the more I think of that Hugo character, the harder I find it to remember that one mustn't speak ill of the dead. If Mike goes to prison, it will be entirely owing to him. But I ought to be ashamed of myself for talking in this gloomy way. Mike's not going to prison, we're going to save him, and we'd better be getting about it without wasting any more time. Is that combination confined to his notebook, or do you know it?'

'I know it.'

'Then away we go, and let me remark in passing that it matters not how strait the gate, how charged with punishment the scroll, I am the master of my fate, I am the captain of my soul.'

It was a few minutes later, as they stood in the interior of the huge safe which was one of Sir Hugo's less harmful legacies to the bank, that Jill uttered an exclamation of surprise.

'Golly!' she said. 'It's hard to realize that this institution is short of money. There's enough in here to choke a horse. We shan't be able to pack half what we want in this little suitcase.'

Ada was busy with bundles of notes. She eyed the suitcase critically.

'It *is* small.'

'We should have brought a steamer trunk.'

'I know,' said Ada, inspired. 'The basement!'

'Where is it?'

'Down those stairs.'

'And what about it?'

'There are some canvas bags there. I'll get them.'

'No, let me go. You carry on with the packing. You're a much better packer than I am.'

'The bags are in the far corner.'

'I'll find them,' said Jill.

She went out, glad to be away from the safe, for it was very stuffy, and she had reached the head of the stairs leading to the basement, when suddenly from somewhere up above came the tinkling of breaking glass, and she stood paralysed. It did not take her more than a numbing second to realize that rivals were invading Bond's Bank, and her first thought was that they must not find it brightly illuminated. Darting to the switch, she pressed it down and in the darkness groped her way back to the stairs and so to the comparative safety of the basement.

She reached it just as Ferdie the Fly, armed with a torch, began the descent from the floor above.

Smithy and his American friend Frank were waiting on the pavement outside for the door to open, and Smithy, whose manners were always excellent, proceeded immediately to congratulate Ferdie in well-chosen words on his skill in climbing to the upper window by which he had entered. It was a feat, said Smithy, which he himself could not have performed to win the most substantial bet. Ferdie replied in suitable terms, and it was in a pleasant atmosphere of mutual esteem that they passed into the main office.

Smithy, like Charlie Yost, gave no outer indication of being a man accustomed to operating outside the law. His long mild face, drooping moustache and clear, honest eyes, peering as did Charlie's from behind horn-rimmed spectacles, combined to present the image of a blameless jobbing gardener who lived in the suburbs, kept rabbits and took the bag round in church on Sundays. On the occasion of his only appearance in the dock even the judge had seemed surprised to encounter an accused with such an aura of respectability, and when sentencing him to eighteen months' imprisonment had done so with almost an apologetic air, as if afraid that he might be taking a liberty.

Frank, with his B-picture face and flamboyant dress, seemed more the stuff that criminals are made of. He favoured bright suits and gleaming, sharply pointed, shoes and, though not connected with Her Majesty's Household Brigade, generally wore a Guards tie. He was considerably younger than Smithy and much more highly strung. Jill at this moment happening to upset some object in the darkness of the basement, he leaped like a salmon in the spawning season.

'What was that?'

Smithy preserved his monumental calm.

'What was what, Frankie?'

'I heard something.'

'You couldn't have done. There's no one here. You're just a little nervous, chum. Bound to be, operating in a strange country. I'd be the same if I was over in America.'

'It's those wigs,' said Frank, wiping his forehead. 'I looked in the other day at that joint they call the Old Bailey, and they were all wearing wigs.'

'You didn't like them?'

'They gave me the willies.'

'Odd. When my law-suit was on at the Old Bailey, I remember thinking them picturesque.'

'It wouldn't take much to make me get out of the game.'

Smithy shook his head disapprovingly.

'I wouldn't. You retire, and what happens? You loaf about the pub turning yourself into a sot, losing your self-respect. No, you stick to your job, my boy, and don't go getting the wind up.'

'What do we do if the cops come?'

'Treat them with silent contempt,' said Smithy humorously. 'But there won't be any cops. The guv'nor has sent them all up to Mallow Hall. You can always rely on the guv'nor. With him behind you, nothing can go wrong.'

Frank was not to be consoled.

'I'd say a hell of a lot had gone wrong. How about that guy Basher including himself out?'

'Even the guv'nor couldn't have foreseen that. And he'll have found someone to take his place.'

'Who says so?'

'I say so. And so will Ferdie, if you ask him. Won't you, Ferdie?' said Smithy, turning. 'Why, hullo, what do you think you're doing?'

Ferdie was bending over the small safe in which Mike kept his personal papers. He had a pot in his hand and was applying its contents to his fingertips. He was looking tense and concentrated.

'I believe I can do it,' he said. 'Yes, I believe I can do it.'

'Do what?'

'Open this safe just by feel. Like Jimmy Valentine. He did it, so why shouldn't I?'

Frank had no comment for this but a snort. Smithy in his gentle way tried the appeal to reason.

'That was just a made-up story, Ferdie. I don't say there might not be some that have done it, but it's a gift, same as poetry. Got to have finger ends that can detect the movement of the mechanism.'

'Maybe I have them. And I've been studying locks. What I don't know about safe locks isn't worth knowing.'

'And what you do know about them isn't worth knowing either,' said Frank sourly.

'What is the argument about?' asked a bland voice, causing Frank to repeat his salmon impersonation and even the phlegmatic Smithy to quiver. Horace was in their midst, a portly figure radiating dignity and responsibility.

Smithy was the first to recover.

'I didn't hear you come in, guv'nor.'

'One takes pains not to be heard, my dear Smithy. What is Ferdie doing with that safe?'

'Trying to open it with his fingertips.'

'And I've done it,' said Ferdie as the door swung open. 'I told you I would.'

If he had hoped to create a sensation, he was not disappointed. Smithy said 'Well, well!' and even Frank was complimentary.

'Boy!' he said. 'With a talent like that, you're going to go places.'

'Yes,' said Smithy, 'we've got to take care of you, my lad. We'd better have that cough of yours seen to.'

'You are certainly revealing unsuspected gifts, Ferdie,' said Horace. 'With the pre-eminent climber of the sides of houses we were acquainted, but this is a new development.'

'Thought I'd like to have something to fall back on, guv'nor, when I got too old for climbing.'

'Quite right. Always have a second string. What's inside?'

'Mostly notebooks.'

'And what we are after is cash. I suppose your talented finger-tips would not act with equal success on the larger safe?'

'No, guv'nor, afraid not. This one's an oldie. You can feel when the tumblers drop. That one's posh.'

'Then we shall have to wait for Charlie.'

'For who?'

'Charlie Yost, Smithy. Ferdie will no doubt have informed you of Basher's regrettable lapse. Charlie is taking his place.'

'But I thought you and him weren't talking to one another.'

'It is true that there was a coolness between us, but recently we were able to find a formula. Ah, this must be Charlie now,' said Horace. His quick ear had heard a footstep.

But it was not Charlie who entered. It was Basher Evans.

11

The main office of Bond's Bank was roomy and could if necessary accommodate quite a large number of clients waiting to be
told that in the circumstances it would be impossible to increase
their overdrafts, but Basher seemed to fill it from wall to wall.

There was no suggestion in his manner, as he entered hum-
ming a hymn tune, that he was expecting an unfriendly reception
– understandably perhaps, for men of his size and muscular
development are generally well received by one and all. His face,
however, was grave, and one could see how much it pained him
to find old friends engaged on an enterprise which could not
but start them off at a disadvantage in the next world. They
would be sorry when they snuffed out and came up before the
judgment seat, he was telling himself, and the only thing you
could say for them was that they did not seem to have got very
far with their wicked work, so that an eleventh-hour repentance
was still possible.

Horace, on his part, though surprised, was not displeased to
see this once valued but now renegade assistant. He assumed that
Basher, thinking it over since their last meeting, had undergone a
change of heart and had come in the hope of being taken back
into the fold. He was not a vindictive man, but the other's
defection had wounded him deeply, and he was happy to be
able to inform him that repentance had come too late, for his
services were no longer required. It was only when Basher spoke
that it was borne in upon him that he had placed an erroneous
interpretation on his presence.

'If you sons of Belial are waiting for Charlie,' Basher said,
ignoring conventional greetings, 'you can pack it up. He isn't
coming.'

Until this moment all conversation in the bank had been conducted in cautious undertones, even Horace moderating his usual fruity accents, but on the word 'coming' prudence was abandoned. Smithy, Frank and Ferdie all said 'What!' simultaneously, and their combined efforts made it virtually a shout.

The sensation he had caused seemed to gratify Basher. He went on with evident pleasure to elaborate his statement.

'No,' he said, 'Charlie won't be here, so don't you think it. I went to see him last night and wrestled with him in prayer. Took a bit of doing, because he wasn't easy to persuade. He was like the deaf adder which, as I dare say you know, stuck its feet in and wouldn't listen to argument. It wasn't till I told him I'd knock his block off if he went anywhere near this bank that he saw the light and promised to abstain from the evil deed he'd been contemplating. He was as sick as mud,' said Basher, lowering the tone of his prose style for a moment.

Frank was perhaps the most moved of Horace's three co-workers. Looking like George Raft and speaking from between clenched teeth, he said he wished Charlie had blown a hole in Basher. It was, he said, what he would have done himself, and Basher said that as a matter of fact it had been suggested.

'But I made him see what an injudicious move it would be. Charlie's got sense, and he knows what happens to you in England if you go about shooting holes in people. It's not like the free and easy way they have in Chicago. It'd be a lifer, I told him, and he saw what a mug he'd be to cop the big one just for the passing satisfaction of rubbing me out. He got the message.'

Horace was standing silent and motionless, as if like Lot's wife he had been abruptly converted into a pillar of salt. The blow had been a shattering one. He was aware, for he had learned the passage at school, that the poet Burns had emphasized that it is advisable always to budget for the possibility of the best-laid plans going wrong – or, as Burns had preferred to put it, agley – but his success until now had been so uniform that he had come to think that nothing in the nature of failure could ever happen to him. He was Appleby, the Guv'nor, the man who was always right.

True, there was the matter of Ada and her refusal of his proposal of marriage. Something had certainly gone wrong there. But that could scarcely be said to count. Gifted men are notoriously unfortunate in their love lives. Look at Napoleon ... Shakespeare ... Doctor Crippen. The fiasco precipitated by Basher Evans had blotted his escutcheon in his professional capacity.

He bore his discomfiture well, as a strong man should. Beneath the bludgeonings of chance his head, like that of Jill's Uncle Willie, was bloody but unbowed. Only a pinkness at the top of it showed how powerfully Basher's pronouncement had affected him. But though he was feeling as if his interior had been churned up with an egg-whisk, his voice was calm and unshaken as he said:

'In that case, boys, I fear that our operation must be postponed.'

'You'll sleep sweeter,' said Basher, nodding approval. 'Well, good night all.'

'Guv'nor!'

The cry proceeded from Ferdie, who had wandered to the big safe as if with a last hope that it might prove susceptible to his fingertips. Horace eyed him dully.

'Yes, Ferdie?'

'This safe's open!'

'Open?'

'Yes, and...'

His voice died away, and he stood staring. Horace revived like a watered flower.

'So we shall not require Charlie, after all, Basher,' he said.

Basher acted promptly. Crossing the room with a speed not often seen in so large a man, he thrust Ferdie aside, and closed the safe door with one powerful thrust of a hamlike hand.

'That'll remove temptation from your path,' he said, smugly, and with a 'Well, good night once again', he was gone. He left behind him a stunned silence. It was broken by Ferdie.

'What I was going to say, guv'nor,' said Ferdie, 'was that there's a girl inside here.'

III

Constant association with him over a number of years had made Horace very fond of Ferdie. He liked him as a person and admired the skill with which he performed his professional duties. In expansive moods he had sometimes said that without Ferdie the whole Appleby organization would have to go out of business.

But frivolity at a time like this, when all his plans lay in ruin about him, was intolerable. The top of his head deepened almost to magenta, and his voice took on a menacing sternness.

'This is no time for joking, Ferdie.'

'But I'm not joking, guv. I saw her. She was laying with her head up against a suitcase.'

'Why would a girl be lying in a safe with her head up against a suitcase?'

'Ah,' said Ferdie. 'I wondered that, too. Struck me as odd.'

It also seemed unusual to Smithy, though he conceded that you never knew what girls would be up to next these days. A more plausible theory, he suggested, was that Ferdie was cockeyed and had been seeing things, a solution which the latter combated heatedly.

'I'm not cockeyed! I'm not seeing things! She's there, I tell you, laying with her head up against a suitcase.'

In spite of himself Horace was beginning to waver. He knew Ferdie to be level-headed and not at all the sort of person to suffer from hallucinations. Incredible as it seemed, there might be something in this extraordinary statement of his. Nevertheless, doubts still lingered.

'But, Ferdie, a bank closes at three o'clock and everybody working in it is away by five. If this girl you say you saw has been there since then, she must be dead. She could not have survived without air, and how long does it take to exhaust the air in an airtight safe?'

'But with the door sort of ajar there would be air coming in, guv. Basher's only just shut it. And she was laying against the suitcase because she passed out in a swoon when she heard it shut, realizing what a spot she's got herself into. The way I see it, she works here, buzzed off at closing time, came back because there was something she'd forgotten, heard us, got scared and hid in the safe. It figures.'

Frank had a word to say to this.

'Figures, my foot. How did she get into the safe?'

'Opened it, of course.'

'How did she know the combination?'

Hard pressed, Ferdie had to think for a moment, but the answer came to him.

'She's probably the boss's secretary or something,' he said, and an icy hand seemed to place itself on Horace's heart. Wishing, if possible, to save the boys trouble when the time for action came, he had made guarded enquiries of Ada, with regard to the combination of the big safe, though without result, for she had been discreetly reticent. She had, however, mentioned that it was known only to Mr Michael and herself, and for an instant the solid premises of Bond's Bank seemed to flicker before Horace's eyes as if a giant hand were shaking them. He clutched Ferdie's arm.

'What did this girl look like?'

Once more Ferdie had to think. Word-portrait painting was not really his forte.

'Well, I only saw her for half a jiffy, guv'nor, but I'd say she was sort of short and stocky. Kind of round face.'

Horace had heard enough.

'Where's the telephone?'

'Over there, guv. Why?'

'I am going to call Mr Bond and get that combination.'

To say that these words caused consternation would be in no way an overstatement. Ferdie gasped. Frank uttered a peculiar sound like a man with catarrh gargling mouth wash. And even Smithy deviated from his customary placidity sufficiently to allow his lower jaw to fall an inch or two as if he had been taking the bag round in church and had seen a worshipper drop a penny in it. But such was Horace's majesty and the authority with which years of leadership had invested him that none of the three made a move to stop him as he dialled. He could not have been more immune from physical interference if he had been Basher.

'Wellingford 834,' said Horace. 'Mr Bond? Good evening, sir. This is Appleby.'

CHAPTER 10

I

Mike was a dutiful nephew, and ever since her accident it had been his practice to look in on his Aunt Isobel as often as he could manage and do his best to cheer her up in her afflicted state. He knew what it was like to be confined to bed with a broken leg, this having happened to himself in the course of his riding career.

Tonight he was late in arriving and was disturbed to find her in an agitated condition quite unlike her usual calm. She greeted him with an impassioned cry which in its timbre might have proceeded from one of the two cats on her bed.

'Where have you been, you blasted boy? I've been trying to get you for hours.'

'Oh, really? I'm sorry. I had to dine with the vicar. Couldn't get out of it. He wanted to cry on my shoulder about the church organ, which apparently needs vitamin shots and top dressing with guano and all sorts of things. But nothing, I told him, that a good village concert won't cure. Why, is something wrong? Your leg been hurting you again?'

Miss Bond uttered a snort which caused both cats to leap from the bed, and even the dachshund opened one eye in mild astonishment.

'Blast my leg! What's all this about the bank?'

'Oh!' Mike gave a little gulp. He had not supposed that this topic would be touched on. 'I wasn't intending to tell you about that.'

'Very considerate of you. Didn't think I'd be interested, eh?'

'I thought it would come as such a shock.'

'It did. It laid me out as flat as a Dover sole.'

'But how did you find out?'

'That guffin General Featherstone rang me up and told me.'

'Damned fool.'

'He said he thought I ought to know that Bond's Bank was on the point of going down the drain and that you and he and Gussie Mortlake were headed for chokey. I couldn't believe it at first. How could a thing like that happen to Bond's Bank?'

'Easily enough with Uncle Hugo running it. He told you about Uncle Hugo sneaking the customers' money to pay for all those benefactions of his?'

'Yes, he didn't omit to mention that.'

'He oughtn't to have mentioned anything. Upsetting you like that, and quite unnecessarily.'

This time the violence of Miss Bond's snort caused the dachshund to open both eyes.

'Did I hear you use the word "unnecessarily"?'

'Yes. Relax, Aunt Izzy, relax. There's nothing to worry about. I can't give you the details, but I've found a way of raising the money I need to put the bank straight.'

'You have?'

'Yes, ma'am.'

'What is it?'

'That's my little secret.'

'You aren't going to tell me?'

'I can't tell anyone.'

'That sounds fishy.'

'It is fishy. But it'll work.'

'So I have to pass a sleepless night trying to think what the hell it can be?'

'That's it. You can be doing your crossword puzzle.'

'And you call yourself a nephew! Still, everything's really all right, is it?'

'It will be.'

'This is official?'

'Absolutely official.'

'Then maybe I shall be able to get to sleep after all,' said Miss Bond, 'though I still think you're a pig not to let me in on it. You know, Mike, I ought to have foreseen something like this. If I've thought once that Hugo was splashing the money about too freely, I've thought so a dozen times. With everything the price it is nowadays you simply can't go strewing libraries and hospitals all over the place. The Rothschilds couldn't do it. But it was no use trying to make Hugo see that. It wasn't in him to listen to the voice of reason. He was one of those men who tell women not to bother their pretty little heads about things they don't understand, and that's what he would have told me if I had uttered a word of warning, not that I have a pretty little head. How much are you short?'

'A hundred thousand, give or take a pound or two.'

'And you can really make that up? It sounds a lot of money to me.'

'I can.'

'God bless you! Now who can that be at this time of night?' said Miss Bond as the telephone rang. 'If it's the General, tell him from me that he ought to be in a home for the halfwitted.'

Mike went to the telephone, listened for a moment, then slammed down the receiver and came away laughing.

'Well, well,' he said. 'Who'd have thought it?'

'Was it the General?'

'No, Appleby. And as tight as an owl.'

'Who's Appleby?'

'The new butler. Didn't you know we had a new butler?'

'Nobody tells me anything. What became of Coleman?'

'He had to leave. Appleby's taken his place.'

'And what makes you think he's tight?'

'He said he was burgling the bank.'

'Burgling the *bank*?'

'Just that. "I'm at the bank, sir, burgling it," he said, and don't ask me what could have put an idea like that into his head. He's probably mopping it up in some pub. Extraordinary the way drink takes people. I read somewhere about a butler who got pie-eyed one night, and the way it affected him was to make him go into the lady of the house's bedroom in the small hours and start piling plates and glasses and knives and forks on top of her. Thought he was laying the dinner table.'

'I knew a man when I was a gairl who came home on New Year's morning and mistook the coal scuttle for a mad dog and tried to shoot it with the fire tongs. Fellow named Fish. He wasn't a butler.'

'We can't all be. But I must say I'm surprised at Appleby hitting it up. Super-respectable he seemed to be. All bald head and polished manners. Wonderful references, too. He was with Sir Rupert Finch at Norton Court in Shropshire before he came to me. I've never met Finch, but I know all about him and he's not the man to take on a butler who wasn't the quintessence of everything a butler should be. Oh, my God, there he is again,' said Mike.

He went to the telephone, prepared this time to stand no nonsense.

'Appleby!' he said in a voice of thunder.

II

His right ear drum momentarily numbed, Horace transferred the receiver to his left. Though shaken to his foundations with horror and dismay, he knew that he must force himself to be calm. This was an occasion when it would be necessary for him to pick his words with care if he was to create in his audience that suspension of disbelief of which dramatic critics write so much. He had always found Mike a reasonably intelligent young gentleman, and reasonably intelligent young gentlemen are apt to be slow in giving credence to their butler's statement that he is burgling a bank. The hand that held the receiver was quivering, but the voice in which he spoke was his customary equable voice.

'I regret being compelled to disturb you again, Mr Bond,' he said, 'but the matter is one of the utmost urgency.'

('What's he saying?' asked Miss Bond. 'Just babbling?'

'Something about something being urgent. And he doesn't sound tight.')

'A very grave situation has arisen and one that calls for your immediate co-operation. I must once more assure you that I and my colleagues are at the bank, burgling it. . . .'

('What did he say then?' asked Miss Bond. 'Fill me in, boy, fill me in.'

'He keeps insisting that he's burgling the bank.'

'Doesn't sound likely. Do butlers burgle banks? You must be wrong about him not being blotto. Is he hiccuping?'

'No.'

'Though that doesn't prove anything. You can be tight without hiccuping. Hugo often was.')

'... and I am sorry to say that your secretary Miss Cootes has become locked up in the larger of the two safes, and unless she is extricated without delay, she must inevitably suffocate.'

'What!' cried Mike, leaping. 'What did you say?'

('What *did* he say?'

'He says Ada Cootes is locked up in the big safe.'

'That nice gairl? Good heavens!')

'In these circumstances I must ask you to be good enough to give me the combination. Every second enhances her peril. Another few minutes and the air will be exhausted...I beg your pardon, sir? I did not catch that. You are coming here at once? I fear you could not possibly arrive in time. It is essential that I have the combination...Sir!...This is disastrous... Think, Mr Bond, think! This is a matter of life and death...Oh!'

Horace's face had suddenly lost its drawn look. As he replaced the receiver, it was as if a bright light had been switched on behind it.

'Mr Bond says he cannot remember the combination,' he said, 'but it is in a red notebook in the small safe, which you have fortunately rendered accessible to us with your subtle skill, Ferdie. Yes, here it is,' said Horace. 'Yes, written down in admirably clear handwriting. Smithy!'

'Yes, guv?'

'You generally carry a flask with you on these expeditions of ours. Have you it now?'

'Yes, guv.'

'Good. The poor girl will need a restorative. What is it? Brandy?'

'Whisky.'

'Whisky will do. Take it into Mr Bond's office. I will be with you in a moment.'

Ada was lying, precisely as Ferdie had said, with her head up against the suitcase which she and Jill had been at such pains to fill with Treasury notes. Reverently Horace picked her up and bore her in his arms across the floor, a slight suggestion in his manner of the well-trained butler bringing the drinks into the drawing-room after dinner. One felt that he would have preferred to be carrying her on a salver.

It was at this point that Frank exploded. Throughout these exchanges he had been giving every indication of mental disturbance – shuffling his gleaming shoes, plucking at his Brigade of Guards tie, starting for the telephone as if to wrench the receiver from Horace's hand and recoiling as his eye met Horace's. Only now did his pent-up emotions find an outlet.

'Hey!' he cried, and Horace paused.

'Something on your mind, Frank?'

'I'll say there's something on my mind. What you going to do with that dame?'

'Restore her to consciousness.'

'And have her see us all and put the finger on us at the line-up. Are you crazy? That guy you were talking to will have phoned the fuzz two seconds after you rang off. It'll only be a couple of minutes before we have them piling in on us.'

'They're all up at the Hall chasing escaped convicts, my dear boy. I saw to that.'

'And I'm seeing to getting the hell out of here without stopping to kiss you goodbye. I'm off!'

Horace was all amiability.

'Certainly, Frank, don't let us detain you if you wish to leave. But if I may offer a suggestion, go out by the basement door just to be on the safe side. There may be someone in the street. Not likely at this hour, but possible. Really, Smithy,' said Horace, as Smithy came out of the office and Frank started to clatter down the basement steps, 'I must say I am a little surprised that you should have recommended someone as neurotic as our late friend. He would do better in some other line of business.'

He passed on into the office and with infinite gentleness lowered Ada into the comfortable chair in which clients sat when calling on the manager. Her eyes were still closed and she was breathing heavily. Smithy's flask was lying on the desk. He reached for it.

Outside, Ferdie stirred uneasily.

'What about it, Smithy?'

'About what, Ferdie?'

'Legging it. Seems to me Frank's got the right idea.'

Among the interesting features of Smithy's physical make-up was his prominent ears. They stood out from his head like the handles of a Greek vase. He was looking now as if he were unable to believe them.

'Ferdie, I'm shocked! Leave the guv'nor flat?'

'But the cops! They'll be here any minute.'

'Not if they're all up at that Mallow Hall place. And even if they came in their ruddy thousands I wouldn't desert the guv'nor in his hour of—'

He was possibly – indeed probably – about to add the word 'need', but at this moment there proceeded from the basement a confused uproar, and Frank reappeared. He was propelling Jill before him with a hand on her elbow.

'For crying out loud!' he said disgustedly. 'Here's another of them. Dames! Butting in everywhere, won't let a man have one thing to ourselves!'

Horace came out of the private office.

CHAPTER 11

I

The basement of Bond's Bank was not one of those cosy nooks where a girl can relax in comfort and let her thoughts drift idly from one agreeable topic to another. It smelled in equal proportions of mildew, old documents and mice, and the ghosts were even more numerous there than in the main office. Already Jill had felt several icy fingers creeping over the back of her neck, and her peace of mind was in no way restored by listening to the sounds that came down to her from above.

Muffled voices were speaking and she could distinguish no words, but the mere fact that there were voices where no voices should have been was sufficient to chill the spinal cord of the most resolute girl. Under conditions such as these not even her Uncle Willie's panacea could serve. The basement was certainly black as the pit from pole to pole, but she was under no illusion that hers was a soul that could be described as unconquerable. It was as of even date a timid and apprehensive soul, rather like that of a nervous rabbit. It was obvious, and had been obvious to her ever since she had heard that tinkle of breaking glass, that hers and Ada's amateur burgling had been interrupted by the arrival of professionals with similar ends in view, and she speculated pallidly as to what was going to happen when they found Ada. What did burglars do to girls they found in safes? Whatever it was, it was bound to be something extremely unpleasant.

Then suddenly, it was as if one of the ghosts, possibly that of the late Sir Hugo in a belated spasm of remorse, had whispered in her ear that she could ease the whole situation by going out through the basement door into the street and summoning the police. It was surprising, she felt, that she had not thought of that before, and she was groping her way to where she supposed the door to be, when Frank made his abrupt descent of the stairs, bumped into her, uttered a startled shout, seized her forcibly by the elbow and propelled her to the floor above, as described.

Blinking in the light, she was for a moment aware only of being surrounded by several men, probably of ruffianly appearance but all indistinguishable. Then, her eyes clearing, she saw Horace.

Not with surprise, for her knowledge of his past was enough to tell her that if dark doings were in progress in Wellingford it was only too probable that he would be mixed up in them, but oddly enough with relief. A criminal he might be and unquestionably was, but there was that about him that inspired a girl with confidence. She felt that she could rely on his chivalry. He seemed to her to look like one of those men who never lay a hand upon a woman save in the way of kindness, and someone of that sort was what, if she had been a literary critic, she would have said that she most desiderated.

Nevertheless, when she addressed him her voice was cold and her manner curt. One may be relieved to see dregs of the Underworld, but there is no need to become chummy with them.

'Good evening, Appleby.'

'Good evening, miss.'

'So I was right in thinking you were the man behind that Norton Court business?'

'It would be idle to deny it.'

'And these are some of your gang?'

'I would prefer to call them co-workers.'

'Won't you introduce me?'

'Certainly. It was remiss of me not to have done so before. First we have ... what name are you using this season, Frank? Ah yes, I remember. This is Mr Fortescue.'

'How do you do? Would you mind letting go of my arm, Mr Fortescue?'

'Let go of Miss Willard's arm, Frank. There is no necessity for any rough stuff.'

To Frank this did not seem to make sense. 'Aren't we going to tie her up and gag her?'

'Next on the roster,' said Horace, ignoring the question, 'Smithy.'

'How do you do, Mr Smithy?'

'Pleased to meet you, Miss Willard. Nice weather we've been having.'

'And Ferdie the Human Fly.'

'So that's how you got up to that window! Good evening, Ferdie.'

'Good evening, miss.'

These polite preliminaries concluded, Jill put the question which was uppermost in her mind.

'But where is Ada?'

'Resting in Mr Bond's private office.'

'So you met her. I wonder you could look her in the face.'

'It was not immediately that I was able to,' said Horace suavely. 'She had inadvertently become locked up in the safe.'

'What!'

'Yes, miss.'

'But the door was open.'

'It became closed.'

Jill was bewildered.

'I don't understand. How did you get her out? You couldn't have known the combination.'

'I telephoned Mr Bond, and he was good enough to supply it.'

'You telephoned Mr *Bond*?'

'It was the only course to pursue. One could scarcely allow the poor girl to suffocate.'

'Why not?'

It was not Jill who asked this question. It came from Frank, standing at the top of the basement stairs, poised for flight. Horace's refusal to allow this intrusive dame to be tied up and gagged had confirmed him in his resolve to dissever himself from the Appleby organization as speedily as possible. Strictly orthodox in his views, Horace's departure from the basic principles of his profession shocked and horrified him. It was, he considered, no way to run a business.

He paused only to deliver a bitter parting speech.

'And Smithy kidded me you were a mastermind!' he said, and with a look of scorn and disgust he clattered down the stairs once more, a disillusioned man.

Smithy removed his spectacles and polished the lenses in silence for a moment.

'I'm sorry, guv'nor. I ought never to have let myself be carried away into thinking Frank was the right man for this job. I thought he'd have more of the pull-together spirit.'

'Quite all right, Smithy. You couldn't have known.'

'Want to know what I think, it's those wigs that sapped his morale. He was telling us about them just now. Seems he went to the Old Bailey and saw all those mouthpieces with wigs on their nappers, and it kind of put the wind up him. They don't have wigs in America, so they came as a nasty surprise. But he shouldn't have deserted you like that.'

'It doesn't matter. There was nothing to keep him here. You and Ferdie had better be running along, too.'

'Sure you won't want us any more?'

'Quite sure. The party's over.'

'Then we'll be saying good night,' said Smithy with relief. 'Good night, Miss Willard.'

'Good night,' said Jill. She spoke absently. Her thoughts were not with Smithy and Ferdie. She was staring at Horace, and her manner was that of one from whose eyes the scales have fallen.

'Mr Appleby,' she said, 'I owe you an apology. I was all wrong about you.'

'Indeed, miss? When was that?'

'When I warned Ada not to marry you.'

Horace started, and a flush spread itself slowly over his face. His eyes glowed with an unfriendly light, and it seemed for a moment that he might forget that he was a man who never laid his hand upon a woman save in the way of kindness. In all her sometimes adventurous life Jill had probably never come closer than at this juncture to having a male hand laid upon her in a spirit far from one of tenderness.

'You see, I didn't like the idea of her marrying someone who might get sent up for five years in the middle of the honeymoon. You can't say it would have been pleasant for her. I told her she ought to have nothing to do with you. I said you weren't worthy of her. How was I to know you were a cross between Sydney Carton and the Chevalier Bayard? I am now one of your warmest admirers.'

Horace heaved a sigh.

'I am gratified to hear it,' he said. 'But I fear your change of mind has come too late.'

Jill would have none of this defeatist attitude.

'Not a bit of it. I'm going to see her now, and I don't think we shall have any more of this nonsense of not marrying you. When I tell her how, to save her life, you phoned Mr Bond for that combination, knowing all the time what you were letting yourself in for, there will be a radical alteration in Ada's outlook. She'll say it's the most wonderful thing she ever heard of and what a lesson to us all not to make snap judgments and condemn people just because they are a little liberal in their views about helping themselves to other people's property. By the way, it would be of assistance if I could assure her that all that side of your life was a thing of the past. May I?'

'You may indeed, miss. Even before tonight I have sometimes thought of retiring while, as the expression is, I was ahead of the game, and I am now convinced that the time has come. I have sung my swan song.'

'Then expect me back shortly with good news,' said Jill.

II

It is proof of the depths of Horace's love for Ada that though Jill's departure left him alone and unobserved he did not immediately go to the safe, pick up the money-laden suitcase and disappear with it from the life and thought of Wellingford at the highest rate of speed of which he was capable. Sydney Carton might have done it, and so might the Chevalier Bayard, but one is proud to say that to Horace Appleby the idea did not even occur. He stood motionless, wishing that the door of Mike's office had been less stoutly constructed, so that it would have been possible for him to overhear what was going on behind it.

He mused on Ada. It had, as we have seen, been her cooking that had first turned his thoughts in the direction of orange blossoms and wedding cake, but his admiration for her culinary skill had been merely the spark that ignited the fuse. Since then he had come so to appreciate her other excellent qualities that he was now more deeply in love than he had been when, taken at the age of twelve to his first pantomime, he had been swept off his feet by the charms of the principal girl playing Cinderella. He was stout, bald and middle-aged, and when a stout bald middle-aged man bestows his heart, it stays bestowed. Without Ada, he was vividly aware, life would be a blank.

It was as he reached this conclusion for perhaps the twentieth time that the door opened and Ada came out, followed by Jill, and one look at Jill's face was enough to tell him that what he would have described as his qualms had been needless. She was wearing the self-satisfied air of a defending counsel whose eloquence on behalf of his client has persuaded a jury to bring in a verdict of Not Guilty. And the last of his misgivings faded away when Ada crossed the floor with moistened eyes and flung herself into his arms with an 'Oh, Horace!' which would have convinced the most dubious.

Jill watched them with a benevolent eye. There was nothing for her to say, she felt, and in any event there would have been no time to say it, for at this moment clattering footsteps sounded on the basement stairs and Smithy and Ferdie burst in.

It would have been plain to the most casual observer that they had much on their minds, and Smithy was prompt to explain what it was.

'Guv'nor,' he said, getting down to what lawyers call the *res* without preamble, 'the cops are here.'

III

It is in times of sudden crisis that men like Horace Appleby are seen at their best. Peril accelerates their thought processes. For perhaps a quarter of a minute he may be said to have been taken aback, as any working burglar might have been by what he had just heard, but the weakness passed and he was himself again, the master planner who thought on his feet and did it now.

'Listen, all of you,' he said, with the ring of authority in his voice, 'and don't make me have to repeat myself, because there isn't time. If you keep calm and follow my instructions, everything will be all right. Smithy!'

'Guv'nor?'

'Sit at that desk.'

'Right ho.'

'Ferdie!'

'Guv'nor?'

'Sit at that other desk. Ada!'

'Yes, darling?'

'Bring a couple of ledgers, and give them pens. And you and Miss Willard sit here with dictation pads.'

'I see, sweetie. So as to make it look as if we were having an audit.'

'Exactly,' said Horace, grateful to Providence for bestowing on him a bride who could not only cook like an Escoffier but was blessed with the quick brain that does not need to have things spelled out for it. 'You and Ferdie, Smithy, be reading out figures,' he said, and as he spoke the door bell rang. 'Coming,' he called. 'Who is there?'

'The police.'

'Just a moment.' Horace opened the front door. 'Oh, good evening, Mr Jessop,' he said, surprise and pleasure at this unexpected meeting with an old friend in every syllable of his fruity voice.

It was on the advice of his brother-in-law Claude that Superintendent Jessop had come to the bank. The advice had been given in the insufferably patronizing manner which always annoyed him so much, but he was able to appreciate its soundness. Informed of his dispatching of most of the Wellingford force to Mallow Hall, Claude had been openly scornful. My dear fellow, oh my dear fellow, he had said, and he had expressed surprise that the Superintendent had not detected the hand of Charlie Yost behind the happenings at the Hall. Surely obvious, my dear fellow. Charlie gets an accomplice to start shooting at this Mallow Hall place, knowing that the first thing the people up there will do is call the police, and having got the coast clear he strolls into the bank and cleans it out at his leisure. If you go there now, you will probably catch him in the act. Don't forget, added Claude as an afterthought, that he will have a gun on him. Would I like to come, too? My dear fellow, oh my dear fellow, you're forgetting that I'm on holiday.

The Superintendent, accordingly, had started off alone. His

thoughts as he went were centred uncomfortably on that gun, and his relief on finding himself confronted not by a miscreant presumably as quick on the trigger as a Dodge City sheriff but by a blameless butler was extreme. This butler's presence mystified him, but fortunately Horace was able to provide a satisfactory explanation.

'Come on in, Mr Jessop,' said Horace. 'You will find us rather busy. The bank examiners will be arriving soon, and Mr Bond wants everything to be ready for them. A regular rush it has been, involving, as you see, some night work. I have to be here about the household accounts. You won't mind our getting on with the work?'

'My dear fellow, oh my dear fellow,' the Superintendent protested, regardless of the law of copyright. 'You've made some additions to the staff, I see.'

'Yes, a couple of old pensioners had to be replaced. The toll of the years, Mr Jessop. None of us get any younger.'

'I never saw book-keepers wearing gloves before.'

'Mr Bond likes the books to be kept spotless.'

Smithy cleared his throat and addressed Jill in the crisp, authoritative way book-keepers have.

'Miss Jones.'

'Sir?'

'Take down these figures. Seven, four, three six, point two nine. Five, nought, three, four, one, point seven nine.'

'Not *quite* so fast, Mr Callaghan.'

'Eight, five, three, two, six, point seven four. Will you add them, please.'

'I already have. Two million, six hundred thousand, eight hundred and seventy-four, point nought two.'

'Correct.'

'She added all that in her *head*?' said the Superintendent, amazed.

'Just a gift,' Horace assured him.

Ferdie had a word to say. Smithy's performance had roused a spirit of emulation.

'Tell me, miss,' he said, addressing Ada, 'are these forward accounts included in the trial balance?'

Ada started. The question had found her unprepared. Her thoughts at the moment had drifted off to Horace and how much she loved him.

'I wouldn't be surprised,' she said, and Ferdie said 'Good, good,' feeling complacently that it would take Smithy some time to top that one.

'Well, I mustn't interrupt you busy people any more,' said the Superintendent. 'Good night to you all. Good night, Mr Appleby.'

'Good night, Mr Jessop.'

'Let's see, when is next contango day?' asked Ferdie.

'Please don't say things like that or I shall have hysterics,' said Jill. 'I hope you found us adequate, Mr Appleby?'

'You were wonderful, Miss Willard, and our two accountants were most convincing. Good night, Smithy. Good night, Ferdie.'

'Good night, guv'nor.'

'And now I think I had better be seeing you home, Ada. You have had a trying evening. You will forgive us for leaving you alone, Miss Willard?'

'Don't mind me,' said Jill. 'And I don't suppose I shall be alone for long.'

She was correct in this supposition. Horace and Ada had scarcely left when a car drew up outside, and Mike came in.

CHAPTER 12

I

Mike, like Othello, was perplexed in the extreme. His was a brain of reasonable strength, but the events of this night had put a strain on it which few brains would have been equipped to bear. A young man who is informed by his butler that he, the butler, is burgling a bank and that his, the young man's, secretary is locked up in the safe and on proceeding to the bank finds there the girl he is to marry apparently playing a part in these peculiar goings-on may be excused for being a little bewildered. He gaped at Jill, and the feeling he had had since his conversation with Horace on the telephone, that all this could not possibly really be happening, became intensified.

'What ... what ... what?' he said.

'Am I doing here?' said Jill. 'I've been burgling the bank, darling. It was your suggestion, if you remember,' she went on, ignoring the soft bleating sound with which he had received the information. 'You practically told me to. You said if somebody did, it would get you out of all your troubles, because the examiners would be baffled and would throw their hand in in despair and go into the hay, corn and feed business. It's perfectly simple, really.'

To this view Mike found himself unable to subscribe, continuing to feel that much still remained that called for explanation. But on one point he was limpidly clear. This girl had taken the most appalling risks for his sake, and he gathered her into his arms and expressed his gratitude in a torrent of words, many of which he would not have thought himself capable.

He was shocked to hear her laugh.

'It isn't funny,' he said rebukingly.

'I was only thinking of the audit.'

'The what?'

She explained about the audit, and Mike agreed with her that Horace had shown great resource, but he expressed once more his disapproval of the whole enterprise.

'Enough to give you nervous prostration!'

'Ada was the one who ought to have had that.'

It came to Mike with a shock that he had completely forgotten Ada. It was her predicament that had brought him here, all anxiety and concern, and in the stress of more immediate matters she had passed from his mind.

'Where is Ada?' he asked, looking at the safe, though reason told him that Jill would scarcely be so nonchalant if she were still inside it. 'Did Appleby get her out?'

'Yes, thanks to you giving him the combination. He left a moment ago to see her home. They're going to be married.'

Mike put a hand to his forehead and was surprised to find that it was not burning in a high fever.

'Going to be married?' he said in a low voice.

'Yes.'

'Appleby and Ada?'

'Yes.'

'You're sure you've got the names right?'

'I don't see why you're so surprised. Naturally Ada loves him. He saved her life at great risk to himself, because how was he to know that you wouldn't instantly denounce him to the police? You didn't, I hope?'

'Of course not. So he really was burgling the bank?'

'Yes, he didn't deceive you about that. He and two charming men called Smithy and Ferdie turned up after Ada and I had filled a suitcase with currency. Are you finding it difficult to take it in that he does that sort of thing?'

'I am a little. It's not exactly what you expect in a butler.'

'He's a very unusual butler. Why are you looking so serious?'

'I was thinking of Ada. I don't much like the idea of her marrying a man who busts banks.'

'Well, you're marrying a girl who busts banks. And he loves Ada and Ada loves him and it's love that makes the world go round, so what's there to worry about?'

'Apart from being a crook, don't you think he's too old for her?'

'Yes I do. That point came up when she was telling me he had asked her to marry him. But she doesn't. And she further denies that he's too bald and too stout. Ada's all right. So are you and I all right. In fact, everything's all right in the all-rightest of all possible worlds, as the fellow said.'

'Yes, that's a comforting thought, but I'd feel still happier if Appleby hadn't got away with all that money you and Ada packed in the suitcase. I was planning to restore it to the depositors in due season. He did take it with him, didn't he?'

'Certainly not. He felt that now that he was getting married he had to give up all that sort of thing.'

'You mean it's still there?'

'Right there in the safe, where we left it.'

'Then let's grab it and rush it off to the house and hide it somewhere.'

'An excellent idea,' said Horace approvingly. 'It is what I was about to suggest myself.'

He was standing at the top of the basement stairs, which he had climbed in his customary silent fashion, and Mike leaped like a lamb in springtime. He was in no condition to hear sudden voices speaking from behind him out of, as it were, the void, and Horace's had had on his sensitive nerves something of the effect of a bomb explosion.

It was left to Jill to carry on the conversation.

'Oh, hullo, Mr Appleby,' she said. 'Did you see Ada home all right?'

'Yes, miss.'

'I was telling Mr Bond about you and her. When he has recovered from having you pop out of traps like somebody in a pantomime, he's going to congratulate you. Aren't you, Mike?'

'Eh?'

'You want to congratulate Mr Appleby, don't you?'

'Oh. Yes. Yes, of course. Congratulations, Appleby.'

'Thank you, sir.'

'There aren't many nicer girls than Ada. I think you'll be very happy.'

'I'm sure I shall, sir.'

'Provided you keep out of gaol.'

'Yes, indeed, sir. That is a *sine qua non*. But I think I overheard Miss Willard telling you that I have retired from business.'

'Was she correct?'

'Quite correct, sir. One must settle down. My former activities would not be at all suitable for a married man. But to revert to the matter of conveying the suitcase to the Hall and finding a hiding place for it there, I think this should be done without delay. The best plan would be for Miss Willard to attend to this, while you and I remain to notify the police of the burglary. A telephone call to the Superintendent at his home is probably the best method. Shall I carry the suitcase to your car?'

'No, thanks,' said Mike more promptly and emphatically than was perhaps tactful. 'I can manage.'

11

After the Superintendent had left him on his mission of inspection Claude Potter had gone to his room and started preparing for bed. With him this was always a leisurely practice, and he was still fully clothed and regarding himself admiringly in the mirror, his invariable practice before retiring for the night, when the door burst open and his brother-in-law made a tempestuous entrance, his demeanour suggesting that he had enough on his mind to disconcert two brothers-in-law. His moonlike face was distorted and his always rather bulging eyes bulged even more than their wont.

'Claude,' he said, speaking with difficulty, 'the bank's been robbed!'

Claude was unquestionably startled, but remembering in time that this was just what he had predicted he had the presence of mind not to gratify his relative by showing it.

'As I expected,' he said.

'But I can't understand it.'

'Surely simple, my dear fellow. I told you how the thing would be worked.'

'But when I got there, everything was in order. They were having an audit.'

'Who were "they"?'

'Two book-keepers, two girls and Mr Bond's butler.'

'What was the butler doing there?'

'Something about household accounts he said.'

'At this time of night?'

'He explained that. They're expecting the examiners in any day, so they were in a rush.'

'How do you know they weren't crooks?'

'One of the girls was Mr Bond's secretary, and the butler is an acquaintance of mine.'

'Then the crooks must have been hiding in the basement till the coast was clear. Well, let's go.'

'Are you coming?'

'Of course. Wouldn't miss it for worlds.'

The Superintendent was relieved. He was not fond of Claude, but he had a great respect for his brains and knew what a useful colleague a man of his experience would be in an emergency like this. He himself was feeling out of his depth, nervously aware that his own experience had not fitted him to cope with evil-doing on a major scale. In his long career as a member of the Wellingford force he had never had to deal with anything more heinous than an occasional case of failing to abate a smoky chimney or moving pigs without a permit, except of course when the races were on with their quota of drunks and disorderlies.

Mike and Horace were waiting for them at the scene of the crime – Mike, like the Superintendent, apprehensive, Horace his customary calm and affable self. Mike was hoping to leave most of the talking to his capable ally, but as the owner of the robbed bank it was obviously his task to open the proceedings, so he did so with as much coolness as he could manage.

'Very good of you to come so promptly, Mr Jessop, and you, Mr . . .' he said, wondering who Claude could be. Presumably connected with the police, he supposed, though looking like something in the chorus line of a touring revue.

'My brother-in-law, Sergeant Potter.'

'From Scotland Yard,' said Horace, increasing Mike's nervousness by some fifty per cent. He had all the layman's awe of that institution. 'Mr Potter and I were fellow travellers on the train a few days ago. He was telling me about life at the Yard. He held me spellbound.'

Mike, too, was feeling spellbound and was thankful that Horace, like Basher Evans's gentleman who made the principal address, seemed to recognize that it was for him to take on himself the burden of the exchanges.

'Mr Bond is lucky to have a Scotland Yard expert on the spot,' said Horace gracefully. 'He will need all the help he can get. Mr Potter mentioned on the train that he was on leave, but I am sure he will give Mr Bond every assistance in his power. Though I fear it will take all his skill to unravel this mysterious affair.'

'What strikes me as mysterious,' said Claude, 'is that the burglary appears to have taken place while you were here,' and it seemed to Mike, whom a guilty conscience had rendered particularly sensitive to nuances of speech, that he spoke coldly.

Horace may have gathered the same impression, but he remained unruffled.

'I was not here, Mr Potter. I and some of the bank employees were working overtime in anticipation of a visit from the examiners. When our work was concluded, I left to escort my fianceé to her home. She is Mr Bond's secretary and had been assisting at the audit. Having seen her home I was annoyed to find that I had omitted to take with me the record of my household expenses and returned to get it. On my departure I had of course locked the door of the bank, so you can picture my amazement when I found that during my absence both safes had been opened and realized that there had been a robbery.'

'How ever do you reckon the fellows got in?' asked the Superintendent.

'A very good question, Mr Jessop. That is exactly what I, too, felt was so mystifying. But we have since discovered that a window on the upper floor has been broken. Obviously one of the miscreants must have been what I believe is called a cat burglar. I understand there are men who can climb up the side of any building. This one would have effected an entry by breaking the window and would then have come down and admitted his accomplices.'

'My brother-in-law thinks that while you were all here doing that audit they must have been hiding in the basement.'

'Very probably.'

'You didn't hear anything?'

Horace smiled an indulgent smile. Not such a good question, he seemed to be thinking.

'They would have taken pains not to advertise their presence.'

'That's true.'

Claude spoke. His voice was still cold.

'What did you do when you got back?'

'I immediately telephoned to Mr Bond, who came hastening hither in his car. He lost no time in informing the police of what had occurred.'

'You were away how long?'

'Possibly twenty minutes.'

'And on your return you found the safes open?'

'Both open as you see them now.'

'And no violent methods had been used?'

'None.'

'Then they must have known the combination.'

'Presumably.'

'How?'

Mike was now sufficiently restored to be able to join in the debate. To say that even now he was at his ease would be an exaggeration, for butterflies in considerable numbers were still fluttering about in his interior, but he was capable of elucidating the point which Claude had raised. It was comforting to reflect that he could do it without deviating from the truth.

'I'm afraid I am to blame there. I kept forgetting that combination so often that my secretary made me write it in a notebook which I keep in the small safe when I pack up for the day. These fellows must have found it. It wouldn't take them long to open the small safe. They must have had chisels or whatever they use. And even if they had forgotten them and left them at home, somebody like Jimmy Valentine could have done the job with his fingertips.'

The Superintendent became suddenly alert.

'Who is this Jimmy Valentine? You think he was one of the gang?'

Claude sighed a weary sigh.

'My dear fellow, oh my dear fellow. Jimmy Valentine was a character in a story by the late O. Henry. I hardly imagine that he could have materialized here tonight. We shall have to seek elsewhere for a suspect. Perhaps you had better leave us to take a look round, Mr Bond.'

'Yes,' said Mike gratefully, 'you don't want us getting in your way while you nose about. I can't offer you a drink, I'm afraid. I don't keep anything here. But you wouldn't take a drink when on duty, would you? One's always being told that in detective stories. We'll leave you, then. Come along, Appleby.'

'Appleby!' cried Claude.

He stood staring at the door as it closed behind them. The Superintendent clicked his tongue regretfully.

'Too bad this should have happened to Mr Bond just when the bank was having difficulties,' he said, and Claude spun round as if the words had been a sharp instrument thrust into his elegant trouser seat.

'What was that? What did you say? The bank's in a bad way?'

'That's what I hear.'

'How did you hear?'

'Well, the story's sort of got around owing to Ivy listening at the door. Very wrong of her, of course, but you can't stop these girls having girlish curiosity.'

'Who is Ivy?'

'The parlourmaid at the Hall. She's walking out with one of my men, and she told him about Mr Bond's troubles and he told somebody else – all in the strictest confidence, of course – and that's how the thing became public property, as the expression is. What happened was that Mr Bond was giving lunch to one of those big financiers you read about, and Ivy waited on them, and when she had served the coffee she listened at the door and Mr Bond was asking this big financier if he could lend him a hundred thousand pounds to save the bank from ruin, and the chap wasn't having any. Turned him down flat, according to the witness Ivy. And now this happens and puts the bank still deeper in disaster. It's what I call a human tragedy.'

Claude laughed an unpleasant laugh.

'It's what I call a human ramp.'

'I don't understand you, Claude.'

'Do you mean to tell me you haven't seen through this little game? I should have thought even a country copper. . . . But I suppose I must make allowances,' said Claude more tolerantly. 'I should have remembered that you don't know about Appleby.'

'Mr Appleby? What about him?'

'I had forgotten the name till you mentioned it. He was the butler at Norton Court, where they had that jewel robbery and I always knew he was the brains behind it. And here he is helping Bond to rob his bank. He certainly gets around.'

The Superintendent gaped at him, aghast.

'Mr Bond! Rob the bank! You're joking, Claude.'

'Don't look so surprised, my dear fellow. It isn't the first time something of the sort has happened. Owner of a country bank finds he's going to be caught short and decides that the way out is to fake a burglary, because how is anybody to tell how much was got away with. "Of course the bank's short," he says when they ask him. "Why wouldn't it be with crooks coming in all the time and helping themselves?" It's just the sort of idea that would occur to a man like Appleby, and he suggested it to Bond. So they were having an audit when you got here? What did you do on arrival?'

'I rang the bell and said I was the police.'

'Giving them just the time they needed to grab ledgers and pens. And of course you didn't suspect a thing. You country coppers!'

'But one of the girls was Mr Bond's secretary.'

'The first person they would have had to square. She got her cut all right. Appleby would have seen to that.'

The Superintendent had no comment to make on this, and even if he had had he was in no condition to make it. A man of stronger personality might have argued, but Claude's reasoning had convinced him and his world had fallen about his head, leaving him stunned. That Mr Bond, bearer of the august Bond name, should have stooped to such behaviour! And that Mr Appleby, whom he had so respected, should have proved to be a wolf in butler's clothing! It was enough to numb the vocal cords of any Superintendent.

As he stood there, he was feeling that he had drained the bitter cup to the lees, but as Claude continued his remarks he found that there was still a drop or two left in it.

'Where is this Mallow Hall where Bond lives?' asked Claude, and, though dizzy, he was just able to reply.

'It's in Mallow, a village near here.'

'Then that's where at this moment there must be a nice little bit of stolen money hidden away somewhere. Tomorrow first thing you must get a search warrant and go through the house from top to bottom.'

Not since the day at the Wellingford races years ago, when as a young constable he had been kicked in the stomach by a muscular pickpocket whom he was endeavouring to arrest, had the Superintendent had the unpleasant feeling that the end of the world had come suddenly and without warning, and, unlike Jill's Uncle Willie, he winced and cried aloud.

'Oh, I couldn't! Mallow Hall! I couldn't!'

'You will,' said Claude firmly, 'and I'll come with you to give you moral support.'

CHAPTER 13

I

Ten o'clock next morning found Mike in his study, waiting for Horace to bring him the breakfast of which he was sorely in need. During Sir Hugo's regime breakfast at Mallow Hall had been rather a formal affair, served in the dining-room to himself, Sir Hugo, Miss Bond and whatever guests happened to be staying in the house, but now that death had removed his uncle and a broken leg his aunt, he preferred to take the meal on a tray in the study.

He was not feeling at his best. He had slept fitfully and what repose he had got had been a good deal troubled by nightmares. His eye-lids, like the Mona Lisa's, were a little weary, and he would have liked to lie back in his chair till the restorative coffee arrived. This, however, could not be done until he had performed a task of top priority – the telephoning to Gussie Mortlake. There must be no delay in telling Gussie to get in touch immediately with the obliging Mr Yost and cancelling their arrangement with him.

He wanted there to be no misunderstanding about this. Although necessity had compelled him to agree to Gussie's suggestion that he allow himself to be shot by Charlie Yost in the leg or arm or shoulder – You name it, I'll plug it – Mike had never liked the prospect. Gussie's prediction that it would be no worse than a bad cold had left him still apprehensive, as had Charlie's statement that he, Mr Yost, had been perforated oftener than a social security cheque without noticing it. It was with profound relief that he now rose and crossed the room to the desk on which the telephone stood.

As he reached it, it started to ring, and a moment later an agitated voice came over the wire.

'Hullo ... Hullo ... I want Mr Bond ... Hullo. ... Is that you, Mike? This is Gussie.'

The information had not been necessary. Only one member of Mike's circle had that strange bleating note in his voice, so like that of a neurotic sheep lost on a mountain side in a mist.

'Hullo, Gussie,' he said. 'I was just going to phone you. What's on your mind?'

The question seemed to have had the worst effect on the last of the Mortlakes. For some moments he merely spluttered, as the sheep he so resembled might have done on swallowing a blade of grass the wrong way. Eventually he was able to speak.

'What's on my mind? I'll tell you what's on my ruddy mind. You know Yost?'

It was a query which most men in his position would not have thought it necessary to make, for Charlie Yost, once seen, was not easily forgotten, but Gussie had his own conversational methods. Mike said yes, he knew Yost.

'What about him?'

'The hound has let us down. He isn't going to do his stuff. After promising that he would plug you free of charge. He phoned just now to say the deal was off. After promising!

Promising faithfully. It's enough to destroy one's faith in human nature. Why the devil are you puffing like that?'

Mike had puffed like that because this news item had revived him as effectively as if it had been a cup of coffee. The breath he had expelled had been virtually a hosannah. He had been none too sure that Charlie Yost would accept the information that his services were no longer needed. He might be one of those conscientious professionals who, when they take on an assignment, allow nothing to stop them from seeing it through. The day, Mike felt, was beginning well.

'What made him change his mind?' he asked.

'As far as I could understand him, a friend of his of the name of Basher persuaded him.'

'That seems to call for footnotes. How does this Basher get into the act?'

'He's got religion.'

'Good for him, I hope he'll end up as a bishop. But I still don't understand.'

Again Gussie became incoherent, but eventually intelligible speech emerged.

'Yost rashly let fall something that roused Basher's suspicions and Basher kept on at him till he'd got the full story of the deal we made. He then told Yost he mustn't plug you, because it would be sinful.'

Mike's interest in the matter, now that the salient fact was established that his arm or leg or shoulder had nothing to fear from the Yost automatic, had become merely academic, but curiosity made him proceed with his enquiries.

'And Yost meekly said he wouldn't?'

'I don't know if he said it meekly, but he said he wouldn't all right.'

'Why?'

'Why what?'

'Why had Basher this mesmeric effect on him? I should have thought he'd have whipped out the old equalizer and filled him as full of holes as a social security cheque. Isn't that the normal procedure for gunmen if you try to push them around?'

'But apparently Basher's about eight feet high and a mass of muscle, and he said he'd beat Yost up unless he did what he was told.'

'I can't see why the fact that a man is large should deter a gunman from letting him have it. Makes him easier to hit.'

'Ah, but someone has been telling Yost what happens to you if you go shooting people in England, and it scared him.'

It had been diverting to keep Gussie in suspense, but the time had come, Mike felt, to do the humane thing and put him out of his misery.

'I see,' he said. 'Too bad. Well, Gussie, I've a little story to tell you which will amuse you. Last night . . .'

A frenzied howl came over the wire.

'Good Lord, man, do you realize the state of nerves I'm in? Do you think I'm in the mood to listen to funny stories? I'm off to that pub where Yost is. There's just a chance I can make him change his mind.'

'But, Gussie—'

The explosion of a violently replaced receiver at the other end of the line cut Mike short. Piqued as a man always is when hung up on in the middle of a telephone conversation, he went back to his chair, and as he did so the door opened and he turned to welcome Horace and his breakfast.

But it was not Horace who entered, it was Jill.

11

Although she was not a breakfast tray, Mike gazed at her without disappointment. She had never looked so bright, gay, blooming and beautiful. A Sultan of the old school, always on the alert for fresh talent for the harem, would have had no hesitation in instructing his Vizier to secure her name and telephone number, and would have been depressed if business had not resulted. She seemed to be combining a spotless conscience with the results of a good facial and the spectacle filled Mike with a sort of awe.

'Women are wonderful,' he said. 'Nothing seems to affect them. Here am I, feeling as if my soul had been put through the wringer and looking like a body that has been several days in the water—'

'You look fine. More like a Greek god than anything.'

'— whereas you could walk into a Miss Universe contest and every judge on the panel would instantly shout "The winnah!" After all you went through last night!'

'Don't give it a thought. I enjoyed it. So what happened after I left?' said Jill.

She sank restfully on to his lap and for some moments his thoughts wandered from the question she had asked. She repeated it.

'Oh, that?' said Mike. 'Just routine enquiries.'

'Who turned up?'

'Superintendent Jessop—'

'I've met him. He's a lamb.'

'— and his brother-in-law, a Scotland Yard man.'

Jill started uneasily.

'That's not so good. I didn't budget for Scotland Yard men.'

'Nor did I. However, everything went off all right. I'm not

saying my hair didn't turn white in a single night, but we got by. Our story was swallowed.'

'Even by Inspector Lestrade?'

'Oh yes, he was quite satisfied.'

'You must have been very convincing.'

'Appleby did all the talking. I've developed a deep respect for Appleby. If ever I burgle another bank, I should like him to be at my side. He gives one confidence.'

'Then all is well?'

'So far. Of course, if the slightest thing slips up, I shall do my stretch behind bars.'

'So shall I. But I shan't mind if we're together.'

'I'm afraid we won't be together. Prisons aren't co-ed.'

'Well, we'll have a wonderful time when we both get out. But nothing's going to slip up. Have you had breakfast?'

'Not yet.'

'Then that's what's making you take the sombre view and talk all this nonsense about going to prison. You'll be a different man when you've fed. Not that I want you to be a different man. You're just right as you are.'

'Have you had breakfast?'

'No, but I don't need it. Love keeps me going. I think of you, my king, and eggs and bacon mean nothing to me.'

'Come and have it with me here.'

'Sorry, I'm booked up. I'm having mine with your aunt. I promised I would go back after I had seen you, so that she could resume telling me what she thought of you. She was furious with you, and you can't blame her. You tell her the butler is burgling the bank and Ada's shut up in the safe, and then you rush off and she doesn't see you again. Naturally she was expecting you to come back and give her a full report.'

'I went to her room when I got home, but she was asleep and I didn't like to wake her. Was she very eloquent?'

'Very. She called you some names which were quite new to me.'

'She has a wide vocabulary.'

'And she used every bit of it. I had to be very firm with her. "Sergeant-major," I said, drawing myself up, "you are speaking of the man I love," and she said, "I know I am, you poor misguided wench, but what does it get you loving him if he doesn't love you?" and I said, "Oh, but he does, and we're going to be married if we can both stay out of gaol." And then I explained the whole situation – about you and me and Ada and me at the bank and Mr Appleby and friends coming in and why Ada was in the safe, and she calmed down considerably. She said I was a gairl of spirit.'

'And so you are,' said Mike devoutly. 'Yes, she was certainly right there. Well, tell her I'll be along directly I can navigate. For the moment I'm incapable of climbing those stairs.'

He returned to his chair and closed his eyes, to open them almost immediately as an invigorating aroma of coffee and kippered herring entered the room, followed by Horace with a laden tray.

III

'Good morning, sir,' said Horace.

A long draft of coffee put Mike in the mood for conversation. He felt that there was much to be talked over with this man. The short journey home on the previous night had been conducted in silence – he in a daze, Horace occupied with his own thoughts.

'Good morning,' he said. 'How did you sleep, Appleby?'

'Reasonably peacefully, thank you, sir.'

'More than I did. Quite a night, wasn't it?'

'Yes, indeed, sir. Very trying to the nervous system.'

'Even to yours? Aren't you used to that sort of thing?'

'Actually, no, sir. I have always been more a planner than an executant. I have seldom played an active part.'

'The brains in the background?'

'Precisely, sir. I suppose I might be described as the poor man's Professor Moriarty.'

'Lucky the Super wasn't a Sherlock Holmes.'

'One rarely finds intelligence of that calibre in the rural districts. His brother-in-law presented a more positive menace. He struck me as astute.'

'Me, too, though you wouldn't think so to look at him. Still, you feel we have got away with it?'

'I see no reason to doubt it.'

'Well, I hope you're right. And may I say that it's nice of you not to have worried me with a lot of questions. Because you must have been fairly curious about last night's goings-on.'

'Oh, no, sir.'

'You haven't been asking yourself what those girls were up to?'

'No, sir. My fiancée explained the circumstances as I was escorting her to her home. I understand from her that the bank is embarrassed by a temporary shortage of funds and by abstracting a certain amount of currency she and Miss Willard hoped to confuse the examiners and obtain a respite or breathing space. I thought it an ingenious idea. Arising from that, I hear I have to congratulate you, sir. Ada tells me that you, like myself, are contemplating matrimony.'

'If all goes well.'

'I am sure it will. There seems to me only one weak spot in our case, the fact that the safe was opened by means of the combination and not with the aid of explosives.'

'Why wasn't it, by the way?'

'The operative assigned to the task was unable to be present. Fortunately, as it turned out, for the blast would undoubtedly have killed my Ada. I shudder to think of it.'

'I don't wonder. There aren't so many Adas around that you can lightly have one of them blown up with dynamite.'

'No, indeed, sir. But if you do not mind, sir, I would prefer not to discuss that aspect of last night's happenings. It makes me feel faint. It is strange that I am so much more affected by her merciful escape than she is.'

'Ada's like that. She takes things in her stride.'

'It is a remarkable gift. I wish I had it myself. But when I think how easily you might have refused to give me the combination—'

'I nearly did. I thought you were tight.'

'Quite understandably. It is not usual for a gentleman to be informed that his butler is burgling a bank.'

'Probably doesn't happen more than once or twice a year. And while on the subject of butlers, I suppose you will be leaving me now that you're getting married?'

'Yes, sir, I would like to give my notice, though regretfully.'

'Shall I be losing Ada, too?'

'I fear so. We are planning to settle down on the French Riviera. In my younger days I was a member of the Duplessis mob who operated on the Côte d'Azur, and I became very fond of those blue skies and majestic mountains. I have my eye on a delightful house in the hills above Cannes which we cleaned out many years ago.'

'That was when you were an executant?'

'Yes, sir, and a very efficient one. You would hardly think it now, but in those days I could climb up the side of a house as nimbly as Ferdie.'

'As who?'

'One of my former associates, known as the human fly.'

Mike coughed. A delicate subject had to be broached.

'I hope you won't think it tactless of me, Appleby, but might I ask a rather personal question?'

'Certainly, sir.'

'Is that "former" really the operative word?'

'Oh, yes, sir, you may rest assured of that. I am definitely retiring from business. I have promised my dear wife-to-be that I will do so, and in any case the difficulty of finding competent safe blowers makes my old profession too laborious to be enjoyable. You would scarcely believe the disappointments I have had. Could I bring you some more coffee, sir?'

'No, thanks.'

'Nothing further that I can do?'

'Not a thing. Unless you would like to phone the Superintendent and ask him how he is coming along with his investigations.'

'Scarcely advisable, I think.'

'Perhaps you're right. Then that'll be all. Thank you, Appleby.'

'Thank you, sir.'

Some twenty minutes later, not relishing the prospect of the meeting that lay before him but more or less fortified by kippers and coffee, Mike went up to see his Aunt Isobel.

IV

It seemed to him as he came into the bedroom that in the difficult art of bringing fermenting aunts off the boil Jill was without a peer. Under her soothing treatment what had been an erupting volcano had simmered down to something an erring nephew could face practically without a tremor. Beyond addressing him as 'You rat' and saying that it was about time he let her see his revolting face again Miss Bond gave no indication of the old fire. In her present mood a child, if fairly stout-hearted, could have played with her.

'Jill says you told her you came to see me last night,' she said. 'I bet you didn't.'

'I did. You were asleep.'

'Considering that I didn't close my eyes all night ... oh, well, let it go. What's this she tells me about you two getting married?'

'A marriage has been arranged and will shortly take place, always provided I don't get jugged. If I do, the ceremony will have to be postponed for a few years.'

'Well—'

'Don't say it.'

'Say what?'

'I was thinking of the old music hall song where the man brings his fianceé to meet his mother and the mother takes a long look at her and says "Poor John! Poor John!" You were just going to say "Poor Jill!"'

'I wasn't going to do anything of the sort. I was about to congratulate you, and with good reason. That gairl's one in a thousand.'

'I would put it even higher than that.'

'Though I don't approve of what she got up to last night.

Good heavens, what is this place, a thieves' kitchen? My brother robs the bank, my nurse robs the bank, my butler robs the bank, my nephew robs the bank, his secretary robs the bank—'

'And you'd have robbed the bank if you hadn't been laid up with a broken leg.'

'Perhaps you're right. The fact is we're all a bunch of crooks, and nothing to be done about it.'

A rather dubious look came into Mike's face, as if he thought that in making this statement his aunt had gone too far.

'I hope there isn't.'

'Meaning what?'

'My thoughts had flitted to the Superintendent's brother-in-law. I have an uneasy feeling that he may do something about it.'

'What the devil are you talking about? What's Jessop's brother-in-law got to do with it?'

'He's a Scotland Yard man. He's spending his leave with Jessop and he blew in with him last night.'

'You don't say!'

'He did, and I don't think he was altogether satisfied with our story, though I told Jill he was, not to alarm her.'

'Well, you're alarming me all right. What was the story he wasn't satisfied with?'

'It was about the combination of the safe. I said I was always forgetting it and Ada made me write it down in a notebook, which oddly enough was the truth. And the burglars found it – that's where the story gets a little thin – and so were able to open the safe without any trouble.'

'Sounds all right to me.'

'I'm not sure it did to him. He didn't say anything, but I had the feeling that the explanation hadn't gone too well. I didn't like the look in his eye. He's one of those new Scotland Yard men – Oxford or Cambridge and the Hendon Police College – and they're notoriously a brainy bunch.'

Miss Bond snorted belligerently.

'To hell with them. Let 'em be brainy. You've nothing to worry about. This son of a bachelor can't suspect you of robbing your own bank.'

'He might if he found out it was on the rocks.'

'Which he can't possibly do.'

'No, he can't, can he?'

'Of course he can't. Not a chance.'

'You're a great comfort, Aunt Izzy. So we just ignore the fellow, do we?'

'Completely. He's no menace. He'll have to settle for the thing being a perfectly normal professional job. Why not? Banks are always getting burgled. It's a wonder nobody ever had a pop at Bond's before.'

'Didn't somebody in the early eighteen hundreds?'

'I believe they did, but it hasn't happened again for over a century.'

'Due, no doubt, to the fact that Appleby wasn't around.'

The mention of that name reminded Miss Bond that she had intended to bring Horace into the conversation earlier. Of all the actors in last night's drama he was the one who most excited her interest.

'Tell me about this man Appleby. It was just like you to engage a crook as a butler. You never had any sense, even as a boy. Obvious criminal type, I suppose?'

'Far from it. Respectability itself. Put him in a shovel hat and gaiters and he would pass anywhere for a bishop.'

'So you say.'

'It's true. Most bishops would look like thugs beside him. You ought to see him.'

'Where is he?'

'In his pantry, I imagine.'

'Probably stealing the spoons.'

'He wouldn't steal a spoon to please a dying grandmother. He's a reformed character. He's retiring from business and marrying Ada Cootes, and they're going to live a spotless life on the Riviera. There's a house he hopes to buy outside Cannes. It has a sentimental appeal to him because he once burgled it, in his youth when he was a member of the Duplessis mob.'

'How dear to my heart are the scenes of my childhood.'

'That's the idea, though I don't imagine he was actually a child at the time, because he speaks of shinning up the sides of houses.'

Miss Bond lay for a moment in thoughtful silence.

'Marrying that nice Cootes gairl, is he?'

'And feels he has to be worthy of her.'

'Purified by the love of a good woman, in fact.'

'You put it in a nutshell.'

Again Miss Bond relapsed into a thoughtful silence. She may have been thinking of the idyllic life in store for the Applebys, Mr and Mrs, but probably not, for when she spoke it was on a more mundane topic.

'That suitcase with all the money in it. Where did you put it?'

'In the cupboard in the study. Why?'

It was with a good deal of emphasis that Miss Bond continued her remarks. It was plain that idle curiosity had not prompted her question.

'I'd shift it, if I were you.'

'Shift it?'

'And like lightning. You say this Appleby is a reformed character, and perhaps for the moment he is, but how if he gets a change of heart and finds that he isn't as purified by the love of a good woman as he thought he was? He might, you know.'

Mike was obliged to admit that this was possible. Many a man who has seen the light is apt to switch it off when the Old Adam starts to come to life in him.

'I see what you mean,' he said.

'You go and get it and bring it here. It'll be safe in my room.'

Mike saw that the advice was sound. Even a back-sliding Horace, however eager for financial profit, would hardly venture into Miss Bond's inner sanctum.

'You're always right, Aunt Izzy,' he said. 'I'll go and fetch it now. It weighs approximately a ton and I'll probably strain my heart lugging it up those stairs, but what of that? If I die in convulsions, it'll be just one more grave among the hills.'

The suitcase, dragged from the cupboard, proved to be fully as weighty as he had said. He had placed it by the desk and was contemplating without enjoyment the prospect of negotiating those stairs in its company, when behind him the door opened and the fruity voice of Horace addressed him.

'Superintendent Jessop and Sergeant Potter, sir,' said Horace.

CHAPTER 14

Between the deportment of the two custodians of the law as they crossed the threshold of the study there was a difference so striking that even the dullest eye could not have failed to notice it. The Superintendent, the first to enter, had the uneasy air of a cat on hot bricks or that of a schoolboy who has been summoned to the headmaster's presence and feels that the impending interview will be fraught with embarrassment. To one who had lived in Wellingford all his life there was something bordering on sacrilege in bursting into the home of the Bonds on a mission such as his. The feudal spirit in the England of today is not the spirit it was, but in backwaters like Wellingford it still lingers, especially when encouraged by someone with the forceful personality of the late Sir Hugo. It seemed to the Superintendent that Sir Hugo's portrait over the fireplace was staring at him with an outraged and rebuking eye, and he reached for his handkerchief and furtively dabbed his forehead with it.

Claude Potter, in sharp contradistinction to his perspiring relative by marriage, was even more than ordinarily perky. He saw himself in a position to dominate the coming scene in a manner never permitted to him at Scotland Yard, where the tendency of his superiors was to see that he kept himself respectfully in the background. Hitherto on occasions like this his freedom of self-expression had always been curbed by the presence of an Inspector who held the view that sergeants should speak only when spoken to.

'Good morning,' he said in a crisp, authoritative voice, taking command of the proceedings from the outset, and the Super-intendent, relieved that the talking was to be done for him by one so much more fitted for the task, took some steps in a backward direction and established himself in Claude's rear, where he stood trying to look small and unnoticeable, a difficult task for a man of his bulk to perform with any success. It is never easy for someone weighing fifteen stone to create the illusion that he is not there.

Mike's attitude inclined more to that of the Superintendent than that of his brother-in-law the Sergeant. He was definitely not at his ease. If the poet Burns had entered the room at this moment and referred to him as a wee sleekit cow'rin tim'rous beastie, he would have been compelled to admit that the descrip-tion fitted him like the paper on the wall.

'Good morning,' he said, considerably surprised that he was able to be so fluent. The advent of these visitors at the current stage in his affairs had left him feeling as he had sometimes felt in his boxing days when struck by a muscular antagonist in the solar plexus. At any other time they would have found him relaxed and debonair, but with that suitcase lying there, out in the open and inviting enquiry, nonchalance was beyond him. The best he could do was to hope that he was not giving too realistic an impersonation of a gangster in a television drama trapped by the F.B.I.

Horace, whose habitual placidity had been momentarily dis-turbed on seeing the suitcase, had recovered his poise and was making for the door, when his progress was arrested by an imperious 'Stop!' Turning, he said:

'I beg your pardon, sir, were you addressing me?'

Claude said he was.

'You wish me to remain?'

Claude said he did.

'Very good, sir,' said Horace, and Claude transferred his attention to Mike.

'I should like,' he said, becoming more official with every syllable and in the absence of an Inspector feeling like a dog let off a chain, 'to run over once again the events of last night. You have no objection?'

If this was all he proposed to do, Mike had no objection whatsoever. So long as the conversation did not drift in the direction of suitcases he was delighted to run over as many of the events of last night as his guest could wish.

'None at all,' he said, hoping he was being hearty enough. 'Carry on, Sergeant, carry on.'

'Thank you.' Claude turned to Horace, who was standing with the air of something stuffed by a taxidermist which all good butlers adopt on these occasions. 'After leaving the bank you say you returned.'

'Yes, sir.'

'And found the safe had been opened.'

'Yes, sir.'

'By means of the combination.'

'Yes, sir.'

'And left open.'

'Yes, sir.'

'Very careless of someone.'

'Yes, sir.'

'But convenient for you.'

'I fail to understand you, sir.'

'You were able to loot it without the help of Mr Yost. It does not require much perspicacity,' said Claude, 'to follow the workings of the plan arranged between you and Yost. You were to lure away the police, he was to go to the bank and rob it at his leisure. But it then occurred to you that Yost was a slippery customer who would bear watching, so you went to the bank to keep an eye on him. For some reason he did not arrive and you found the combination and realized that you could do without him. Simple, my dear fellow, quite simple.' Horace was plainly astounded. A butler, no matter what the provocation offered, seldom raises his eyebrows more than a quarter of an inch, but his had shot up to fully twice that altitude. One would have said that his breath had been taken away, had he not spoken.

'Are you joking, Mr Potter?'

'I am not joking, Mr Appleby.'

'Then,' said Horace with icy dignity, 'I shall be compelled to Take Steps.'

Many men, awed by the majesty of his demeanour, would have quailed. Claude merely laughed that nasty laugh of his. Life at Scotland Yard toughens the moral fibre.

'Splendid, Appleby! Just the proper note of righteous indignation.'

'The courts of England realize that a butler's most precious possession is his good name. His livelihood depends on it. You have accused me – before witnesses – of being a criminal. You have impugned my honesty, and I cannot allow it to pass. Mr Potter, you will hear from my solicitors.'

It was at this moment that the telephone rang.

The sudden noise, coming at a time when all Nature seemed to be listening in awed silence to the tremendous words just recorded, had the effect of stiffening Mike in every limb, and it was Horace who moved to answer the summons. He did not, however, get far, for once more an imperious 'Stop!' halted him in mid-stride.

'I will take all calls,' said Claude, picking up the receiver. 'Yes? Who is speaking? Mr who? Yes, he is here. Mr Mortlake wants you, Mr Bond,' he said, satisfied that nothing sinister was to be feared from that source. He had heard his brother-in-law speak of Mr Mortlake as a capable cricketer and some sort of relation of the Chief Constable of the county. Obviously not the kind of man to be mixed up in criminal activities.

'Hullo, Gussie,' said Mike in a voice which only the most insensitive could have taken as having the note of welcome in it. He was feeling that all he needed at a time like this was a chat with Augustus Mortlake.

'I say,' said Gussie. 'Who was that?'

'Who was who?'

'The chap I was speaking to. It wasn't that butler of yours, was it?'

'No.'

'I thought not. Not the same voice at all, and he didn't call me sir.'

'It was somebody who came to see me about something.'

'What?'

'What?'

'What did he come to see you about?'

'Oh, just something.'

'I see. Not that it matters.'

'No.'

'Why I called, Mike, was that I've a wonderful bit of news for you. It'll make your day. You remember Yost?'

'Oh, get on, Gussie. I'm in conference.'

'With the chap?'

'What chap?'

'The chap I was speaking to.'

'Yes, yes, yes! What is it, Gussie? What do you want?'

'I'm trying to tell you, only you keep interrupting. Can you manage to be at home today at twelve sharp?'

'It's nearly that now.'

'So it is. Well, can you?'

'Yes, I'm not going anywhere. Why?'

'Because at twelve sharp a fellow named Frank Fortescue will be clocking in to plug you.'

'What!'

'Yes. He's a friend of Yost's, and Yost has farmed out the job to him. Extraordinarily decent of the Fortescue chap to oblige and extraordinarily decent of Yost to take the trouble to rope him in, and so I told him and he said he'd been terribly worried by the thought that he had let us down and was only too bucked to be able to fix everything up. You'll have to slip this Fortescue character a little something, of course, as you can't expect him to do it free like Yost, because after all he isn't a pal of yours as Yost was, but you can work all that out with him later. Oh, and I nearly forgot to say, the Fortescue will be calling at the back door not the front, because Yost, who has apparently been to the Hall, though what took him there I can't imagine unless he came on one of the days when it's open to the public on payment of two bob or whatever it is, told him there was better cover there. Bushes and things. He'll naturally want shrubbery of some sort to disappear into after doing the job. And don't worry about Fortescue not plugging you in some spot where it won't matter. Yost tells me he's a capital shot. Well, that's that,' Gussie concluded. 'Don't forget. Back door. Twelve sharp. So long.'

If there was one thought uppermost in Mike's mind as he came away from the telephone, it was that, however he passed the remainder of the morning, he would take particular pains to stay away from back doors. He was also musing in no friendly fashion on Charlie Yost. Charlie Yost, he considered, had been extremely officious and meddlesome. Why the man could not have left things as they were, with everybody happy and comfortable, he was at a loss to understand. It was the Charlie Yosts of this world, he reflected bitterly, who upset and complicated everything and caused harmless well-meaning people like himself to feel as if all the muscle had been removed from their legs and a cheap asparagus substitute inserted in its place. He tottered to a chair and sank into it, and Claude resumed his exchanges with Horace.

'You were speaking of your solicitors, Appleby.'

'I said you would hear from them. They will instruct counsel, and when the case comes to court the first question counsel will ask you as you sit in the witness box is How am I supposed to have obtained the combination of the safe?'

'To which I shall reply that you got it from your accomplice Bond. You surely don't imagine that I am so simple as not to know that you and he were in this together. My dear fellow, oh my dear fellow. Really!' said Claude, and Mike leaped in his chair with the abandon of a Mexican jumping bean. Once again he had the disagreeable illusion that he had received a powerful body blow. There was a mist before his eyes, in the centre of which Claude Potter seemed to be flickering like a character in one of the early silent motion pictures.

Horace appeared unmoved.

'Counsel will then ask Why should Mr Bond wish to rob his own bank?'

'And my answer will be because it was on the verge of ruin and he hoped that a burglary would explain the monetary shortage.'

'Mr Potter, your imagination amazes me.'

'Me, too,' said Mike, unexpectedly finding speech. 'Of all the weird ideas! Of all the wild accusations! Of all the libellous—'

'Slanderous, sir.'

'Thank you, Appleby. Of all the slanderous—'

'Imputations, sir.'

'Thank you again, Appleby. Of all the slanderous imputations I ever heard, this one takes the biscuit. Who are your solicitors, Appleby?'

'Bodger, Bodger, Bodger—'

'Good.'

'– and Bodger.'

'Still better,' said Mike, as if feeling that when you get four Bodgers, you've got something. 'Efficient, are they?'

'Extremely, sir.'

'Then you will shortly receive from Bodger, Bodger, Bodger and Bodger not one but two communications, Mr Potter.'

'I shall look forward to it,' said Claude, 'and in the meantime I will be going through the house to find the stolen money. You have the search warrant, Ernest?'

'Yus,' said the Superintendent, his first and only contribution to the debate.

'Then let us . . .'

The sentence remained unfinished. A sudden eager light had come into Claude's eyes, closely resembling that which sometimes came into the eyes of Mike's Aunt Isobel when she solved a clue in her crossword puzzle. His hand rose as if to stroke his small and unpleasant moustache, but what it actually did was point a finger at an object on the floor.

'*What's in that suitcase?*' he demanded. 'Open that suitcase!' he added, and in a voice so loud and ringing that even Horace gave a little jump, while Ivy the parlourmaid, who had appeared in the doorway, was obliged to repeat the observation she had just made. Her first attempt to engage her employer's attention had been rendered inaudible.

'There's a gentleman at the back door wants to see you, Mr Bond,' said Ivy.

Claude started or, as the book of synonyms would have put it, moved with an involuntary twitch or jerk. He had had his suspicions of people who telephoned the man Bond, but they were mild compared with his distrust of those who wanted to see him at back doors. His eyes, already keen and purposeful, became keener and more purposeful. Things, he felt, were moving. He did not actually say 'Yoicks!' or 'Tally-ho!', but these ejaculations were implicit in his manner.

'*I* will see the gentleman,' he said curtly. 'Kindly remain where you are, Mr Bond.'

Mike had leaped to his feet. He had no reason to feel affection for Claude Potter and would never have asked him to come and stay at the Hall or go with him on a long walking tour, but he was humane.

'Don't go!' he cried. 'As a favour to me don't go!'

Claude permitted himself a short, sharp, unmusical laugh.

'In my official capacity I fear I am not able to do people favours, Mr Bond.'

As the door closed behind him, Horace coughed.

'Is the gentleman who has left us really your brother-in-law, Mr Jessop?'

'Yus.'

'You have my sympathy.'

'And mine,' said Mike.

'I found him brusque,' said Horace. 'His manners had not that repose that marks the caste of Vere de Vere. Will he be with us for an extended stay?'

'Two weeks.'

Mike shook his head.

'I doubt if he'll be staying as long as that,' he said, and as he spoke there came, muffled by distance, the sound of a shot. It drew from the Superintendent an agitated 'Coo!' He dashed from the room, as far as it was possible for a man of his build to dash, and Horace followed him at a stately amble.

Mike sank back in his chair with his eyes closed. Over in the corner the grandfather clock was striking twelve.

CHAPTER 15

It was some ten minutes before Horace returned. When he did so, he was alone.

'You must forgive my delay in coming to apprise you of what has occurred, sir,' he said. 'The girl Ivy was having hysterics and water had to be thrown in her face. This took time.'

'Never mind about Ivy.'

'No, sir. She is, as you suggest, merely a side issue. I should like, however, to add that she is now completely restored, though wet. Well, sir, I fear we shall not be able to enjoy Sergeant Potter's society for some little while.'

'He isn't dead?'

'Not quite that, sir, but he has sustained an unpleasant flesh wound which will limit his social activities for a week or so. The Superintendent has taken him to the hospital in his car. We used one of my shirts to staunch the flow of blood.'

'There was a good deal, I suppose?'

'Sir?'

'Blood.'

'There was indeed, sir. To borrow a phrase from Mr Bernard Shaw's Admirable Bashville, he was total gules.'

'Where was he hit?'

'At the back door, sir.'

'I mean where?'

'Oh, excuse me, sir, I misunderstood you. In the fleshy part of the right upper arm. Painful, of course, but not dangerous.'

'No worse than a bad cold.'

'Sir?'

'Nothing. And let's face it, Sergeant Potter was just the sort of man who was asking for an experience like that.'

'I thoroughly concur, sir. I really do not think I ever met anyone to whom I took such an instinctive dislike. Though that peremptory manner of his is, so friends have told me, universal at Scotland Yard. It comes, one supposes, from mixing so much with the lower type of criminal. Would you care for a drop of brandy, sir?'

'No, thanks.'

'It tunes up the nervous system.'

'My nervous system is all right. Though it wasn't when he started to show an interest in suitcases.'

'It was certainly an awkward question he asked at that juncture. It would have been difficult to find a satisfactory reply. One cannot help feeling that the incursion of Ivy was providential. One has the sense of having been, as one might put it, *protected*.'

'Our guardian angels were certainly on the job there.'

'Yes indeed, sir. With, if I may use the expression, bells on. I find myself puzzled, however, to account for the sudden arrival of this mystery marksman. How had Sergeant Potter incurred his displeasure? How did he know Sergeant Potter was here? And why, if Sergeant Potter was his objective, did he ask to see you?'

Mike hesitated. Every man has his little secrets which he would prefer to keep to himself, and this was one of his. On the other hand the events of last night, followed by the events of this morning, had left him feeling that this was a special case. He and Horace had become, as it were, linked by imperishable memories like boys of the old brigade who have stood steadily shoulder to shoulder. He decided to tell him all.

'I can explain that. Potter wasn't his objective. I was.'

'You, sir?'

'Yes. It's a long story, but I'll condense it as much as I can. I'm insured at Lloyd's for a large sum against being injured with intent to kill, and this man came to shoot me, not with intent to kill, of course, but what would have looked like it. All the arrangements were made through a friend of mine, so the man had never seen me. He plugged what he thought was me. It was the only way I could think of for raising money to save the bank.'

It was not the slight dishonesty of the scheme that made Horace shake his head, but doubt as to its chances of success.

'It would never have worked, sir.'

'You think not?'

'These insurance companies can wriggle out of anything. They would have claimed it was an accident.'

'Perhaps you're right. Anyway, I'm now in a pretty awkward position. If I return the suitcase money, the bank will go down the drain. If I don't, I'll go to prison. Potter will spread his suspicions, investigations will be made, and the truth will come out.'

'It is quite a dilemma, sir.'

'Quite. I can't help feeling sorry that man didn't aim more to the left and get Potter in the head.'

'Of all sad words of tongue or pen the saddest are these – It might have been. But I have a suggestion to make, sir, which I think may—'

The opening of the door interrupted him. Ivy appeared, fairly dry now but still not quite the gay carefree Ivy who appealed so much to Sergeant Herbert Brewster of the Wellingford police force.

'Oh, Mr Appleby,' she said. 'Two gentlemen.'

'That sentence surely needs a verb, my dear. What about these two gentlemen?'

'They're waiting to see you, Mr Appleby. I've shown them into your pantry. A Mr Smithy and a Mr Ferdie.'

'Of course,' said Horace, enlightened. 'Two of my former colleagues, sir. I asked them to call. If you will excuse me for a moment.'

He had scarcely left, when Jill came in.

'A message for you, my dream man,' said Jill. 'A near relative of yours is curious to know what has happened to you. Correction. Her actual words were "Go and find out what the devil has happened to that half wit." Apparently you were supposed to bring that suitcase to her room, but the minutes have crept by and still no suitcase. Why the delay?'

'I had visitors. Superintendent Jessop and his brother-in-law Sergeant Potter of Scotland Yard. Jill, darling, I'm afraid things aren't looking too good.'

The light died out of Jill's face. Her lips parted as if she were about once more to try her Uncle Willie's panacea, but all she said, in a small voice, was:

'Go on. I can take it.'

It was not easy for Mike to tell his story, but he managed it. When he had finished, the voice in which Jill spoke was even smaller.

'Oh, Mike,' she said. 'So we're right back where we started.'

'Right back.'

In the long unhappy silence that followed Horace came in, escorting Smithy and Ferdie.

Mike eyed them sourly. He had been about to take Jill in his arms and try to comfort her, and he resented these intruders. He had not supposed that Horace would return, and he had certainly not expected that if he did return he would bring friends with him.

He also resented what seemed to him the smugly cheerful look on Horace's face. It was, he thought, the look of one who is telling himself complacently that however black as the pit from pole to pole might be the depths that covered others he personally was sitting pretty. Horace, he felt, was gloating over the idyllic life to come on the hills outside Cannes and giving little if any attention to the bleak future that lay before Michael Bond. It was not, he considered, the way one boy of the old brigade should behave towards another boy of the old brigade after a night of standing shoulder to shoulder, and if he had been asked at that moment to sum up Horace Appleby in a few words, he would have described him as a fat callous insensitive slob.

Horace, unaware of this silent critique, was genially performing the introductions.

'May I present, sir, Mr Montgomery Smith and Mr Ferdinand Ripley. Miss Willard they have already met.'

'How do you do, miss,' said Smithy in his gentlemanly way. 'No ill effects, I hope, from last night?'

'A few, Mr Smith.'

'I am sorry to hear that, miss.'

'I am a little depressed.'

'Dear, dear.'

'Appleby,' said Mike, shifting uneasily in his chair as if troubled by ants, 'I don't want to seem inhospitable, but could you please leave Miss Willard and me alone for a while? We have a good deal we want to discuss.'

'I can readily imagine it, sir,' said Horace, checking Ferdie with a gesture as he seemed about to join in the conversation, 'but if you will bear with me for a moment, you will find that this is no idle social call. We have a business proposition to place before you, and Mr Smith and Mr Ripley have appointed me as their spokesman. I may speak for you, Smithy?'

'That's right, guv.'

'And for you, Ferdie?'

'Not half.'

'Then I can proceed. You may recall, sir, that when Ivy came to inform me of the arrival of my ex-colleagues I was saying that I had a suggestion to make with regard to the unfortunate position in which you find yourself. Bond's Bank is short of funds, and my friends here and I feel very strongly that this is a situation that should not be allowed to continue. We propose, therefore, to contribute a sum of money which will cover the deficiency and establish the bank once more on a sound footing.'

Mike was having the oddest dream. He seemed to be in his study brooding bitterly on the impossibility of obtaining enough money to save his bank from ruin and himself from prison, and in the strange way in which things happen in dreams Horace Appleby had suddenly appeared and offered to straighten everything out. It was all extraordinarily vivid, and after a short dizzy spell he realized that the reason for this was that it was actually happening.

The first thing he felt was a thrill such as he had never felt before. It was as if the chair in which he sat had abruptly become electrified. Somewhere out of sight an orchestra was playing soft music and the air was heavy with the scent of roses and violets sprouting through the floor.

But then followed almost immediately the reaction. He

remembered the size of what Horace had called the deficiency, and the orchestra became suddenly muted, while the roses and the violets withered on their stems.

'Appleby,' he said, 'I don't know how to thank you—'

'No need to thank me, sir.'

'– and you, gentlemen. But when you hear what the sum amounts to . . .'

'Perhaps you would be good enough to inform us, sir.'

'Roughly a hundred thousand pounds.'

'That seems to present no difficulty.'

'No *difficulty*?'

'It is about the figure I had estimated. You remember me saying so to you, Smithy?'

'That's right, guv.'

Mike was still tottering. His voice came out in a croak.

'But a hundred thousand pounds!'

'Quite within our means, sir. Smithy?'

'I'm good for twenty-five thou'.'

'Ferdie?'

'Me, too.'

Horace beamed on the two financiers like a governess whose pupils have given the right answer to some searching question concerning the principal rivers of England or the hides, tallow and hemp which so many countries seem to be so fond of exporting.

'Smithy and Ferdie have always relied on me to advise them about their investments, and I was able to assure them that their money and interest would be safe with Bond's Bank. And if you are asking yourself "What of the remaining fifty thousand?", I shall be delighted to contribute that. We have all been doing extremely well for many years, sir, and we have lived thriftily.

I have my modest nest egg, and I suppose Smithy and Ferdie are two of the wealthiest burglars in England.'

'Thanks to you, guv,' said Smithy, and Horace simpered a little.

'Smithy is one of my fans. As the French say, more royalist than the king. Then we may regard the transaction as settled, sir. I will get together with you at your convenience and we will see to the drawing up of the papers. For the moment it must stand as a gentleman's agreement. Then that, I think, is all, sir.'

'All,' said Jill, 'except to tell you, Mr Appleby, that you are an angel in human shape.'

'Thank you, miss.'

'So are you, Mr Smith.'

'Thank you, miss.'

'And you, Mr Ripley.'

'Always happy to oblige, miss.'

'I second that motion,' said Mike, 'but I make one reservation.'

'Sir?'

'That's the one. I simply refuse to have you calling me Sir all the time. Good heavens, Appleby, do you realize what you've done for me? You've saved my life. Do you think I want to be called Sir by . . . how shall I describe you?'

'A woolly baa-lamb?' suggested Jill.

'Exactly. By a woolly baa-lamb the hem of whose garment I ought to be kissing.'

Horace was visibly affected. For the first time in thirty years a blush reddened his cheeks.

'My dear fellow, oh my dear fellow,' he said.

THE END

TITLES IN THE COLLECTOR'S WODEHOUSE

Blandings Castle
Carry On, Jeeves
The Clicking of Cuthbert
Cocktail Time
The Code of the Woosters
The Coming of Bill
A Damsel in Distress
Do Butlers Burgle Banks?
A Gentleman of Leisure
Heavy Weather
Hot Water
Jeeves and the Feudal Spirit
Jeeves in the Offing
Jill the Reckless
Joy in the Morning
Laughing Gas
Leave it to Psmith
The Little Nugget
Lord Emsworth and Others
The Luck of the Bodkins
The Mating Season
Meet Mr Mulliner
Money in the Bank

Mr Mulliner Speaking
Much Obliged, Jeeves
Mulliner Nights
Piccadilly Jim
Pigs Have Wings
Psmith in the City
Quick Service
Right Ho, Jeeves
Ring for Jeeves
Something Fresh
Spring Fever
Summer Lightning
Summer Moonshine
Thank You, Jeeves
Ukridge
Uncle Fred in the Springtime
Uneasy Money
Very Good, Jeeves!
Young Men in Spats

This edition of P. G. Wodehouse has been prepared from the first British printing of each title.

The Collector's Wodehouse is printed on acid-free paper and set in Caslon, a typeface designed and engraved by William Caslon of William Caslon & Son, Letter-Founders in London around 1740.